A FLOWER SO FALLEN

A MARY ANN LITTLE MYSTERY

JOSEPH L.S. TERRELL

BellaRosaBooks

BellaRosaBooks

A FLOWER SO FALLEN
ISBN 978-1-62268-139-6

Copyright © 2018 by Joseph L.S. Terrell

Lines from the play *Boeing, Boeing* by Marc Camoletti used by permission.

First Printed: May 2018

Library of Congress Control Number: 2018942469

Also available as e-book: ISBN 978-1-62268-140-2

Cover illustration and design by Roo Harris and Taylor Harris.
Author photograph by Veronica Moschetti - Paris.

Book design by Bella Rosa Books

Printed in the United States of America on acid-free paper.

BellaRosaBooks and logo are trademarks of Bella Rosa Books

10   9   8   7   6   5   4   3   2   1

This book is dedicated to my four blessings: Michael, Emily, Jennifer, and Christopher.

Acknowledgments

Thanks to Amber Bodner Griffith of Dare Coalition Against Substance Abuse (Dare CASA) and to pharmacist J.E. Mertz for their knowledge and help in defining for me the drug problem at the Outer Banks and elsewhere; and to first manuscript readers Cathy Kelly and Veronica Moschetti Reich for their editorial suggestions and critiques. A special thanks, also, to professional editor and writing coach Beth Terrell for invaluable assistance in helping make this a better story. Once again, I want to express my appreciation to publisher Rod Hunter of Bella Rosa Books for his continuing faith in me as a writer.
—*JLST*

A FLOWER
SO FALLEN

CHAPTER ONE

Mary Ann Little bought new pajamas.

The pajamas weren't all that fancy. But they were cotton and looked comfortable. Light blue with a subtle design of some type of pink flower every few inches. She picked up a second pair and thought about buying them since Belk department store offered a second pair at forty percent off.

But she decided against it. No sense in being too extravagant. Besides, one nice pair would be . . . well, that would be sufficient.

Elise Duchamp, with whom Mary Ann had come to the Outer Banks, appeared beside her and pointed to the second pair that Mary Ann still held in her hand. "Go ahead and get two. They're on sale."

Mary Ann put down the second pair as if it had suddenly become too warm to handle. "I haven't paid for these others yet."

Elise turned to the rack of nightwear behind her and pulled out a hanger with a filmy, see-through nightgown with an equally see-through little top. "This is what you need," she said. Elise got that lopsided little teasing grin of hers. "You know Thaddeus would like this."

Mary Ann tucked her chin in and gave the tiniest shake of her head. "Pajamas," she said. "And he's not going to see these. Thaddeus Sinclair is my boss, my editor. Nothing else." But she did add softly, more to herself, "Well, maybe a friend, too."

Elise shrugged and re-hung the gown. "Yeah, sure."

Mary Ann switched the conversation. "Did you get what you wanted in cosmetics?"

"Nope. They didn't have it. But I got some body lotion." She held up a small package. "Keep myself greased up." She winked at Mary Ann. "You never can tell."

Mary Ann cast her eyes upward.

Then Elise glanced at her watch. "We'd better move along. Go ahead and pay for your granny pajamas and we'll go. I want us to get decent seats."

Mary Ann approached the cashier, but with an aside over her shoulder, she whispered to Elise, "They're not granny pajamas."

"Whatever," Elise said.

The cashier, a dark-haired, smiling young woman who scanned the pajamas, said, "They're nice. You don't want a second pair? Forty percent off."

Mary Ann returned the young cashier's smile, and said, "No thanks. Just the one."

"Do you have a Belk card? Another discount if you do."

"Visa," Mary Ann said.

After the transaction, Mary Ann and Elise strode to the front of the store. They passed the brightly lit cosmetic section and once again Mary Ann felt enveloped in the heavy, clinging perfume scents. When they stepped through the automatic doors into the fall sunshine, Mary Ann took a deep, grateful breath.

Elise led the way to her bright red Mustang, parked only three spaces away. As they approached the car, a young man in knee-length shorts and baggy T-shirt got out of a pickup truck he had pulled in next to Elise's car. He started toward the shops there in Dare Centre. An intricately designed tattoo adorned his lower right leg, and he wore his hair in a short ponytail. He eyed Elise.

Elise, her keys in her hand, returned a hint of a smile.

He slowed his steps and turned his head to look again at Elise. She appeared oblivious to his admiring attention, but Mary Ann knew she wasn't.

"He looks familiar," Mary Ann said as she slipped into the passenger seat. She looked over her shoulder, trying to figure out where she might have seen him. His face didn't ring any bells. Maybe it was the tattoo.

Elise made a noncommittal little toss of her head and didn't say anything.

They got in the Mustang and drove south on Highway 158. It was known as the Bypass, but was cluttered on both sides with stores, restaurants, discount souvenir shops, fast food places, surfboard outlets, and just about every other kind of business. It was only one of two north-south roads on the Outer Banks. The other was Highway 12, or Beach Road, and ran parallel to the Bypass. The Atlantic Ocean practically brushed up against the Beach Road in places.

Contrary to her usual driving habits, Elise kept to the posted speed limit of fifty, except for one stretch that dropped to forty-five, which no one, including Elise, seemed to observe.

With one hand on the steering wheel, Elise checked her watch again.

"We've got plenty of time," Mary Ann said.

They were on their way to Manteo to see the Theater of Dare's matinee production of Monty Python's rollicking musical comedy *Spamalot.*

"We made good time coming down," Elise said.

"I'll say." Mary Ann kept her eyes on the road, watching for cars easing onto the five-lane Bypass from the side roads or in the center turn lane waiting to turn left or work back into the southbound traffic. Not that she didn't trust her friend's driving, but Elise was—how to put it kindly?—distractible. "Less than forty-five minutes getting down here from home," she said.

"Home" was the tiny town of Camford Courthouse, north of the Outer Banks beaches.

"I'm really interested to see whether they can pull this show off. It's a difficult one . . . music and everything, large cast," Elise said.

"You're not thinking of trying to produce this show, are

you?"

With a sharp shake of her head, Elise said, "Oh, no. Good as we are, this show's too ambitious for us." Elise, in addition to being very active in a one-person real estate business, was director and manager of the Tracks Community Theater in Camford Courthouse. The full name of the theater was The Other Side of the Tracks Community Theater. The old passenger train depot had been turned into an upscale theater, thanks to donations from the town's citizens, and especially the financial backing of Mrs. Justine Willis Gregory.

At Whalebone Junction, they swung to the right, headed toward the Washington Baum Bridge over Roanoke Sound and into Manteo.

Elise found a parking space right in front of the College of the Albemarle and they entered and bought tickets from one of two women sitting behind a table near the auditorium entrance. Mary Ann and Elise got seats in the middle of the second row.

Elise nodded toward their seats and said, "Good."

Mary Ann scanned the auditorium. Her friend Becky had mentioned planning to see the matinee performance of the play, and they might at least exchange a wave before the show started. But the lights were beginning to dim, and she saw no sign of her friend. Mary Ann frowned. Lately, this had happened a lot. Becky would say she was going to do something, only to fail to follow through.

The apparent head of the troupe stepped onto the apron of the stage and gave welcoming remarks. He cautioned to turn off cell phones and no flash photographs. He stepped away.

Then the auditorium lights dimmed, music swelled, and the curtain rose.

Mary Ann smiled in anticipation.

The show, a broad parody of the King Arthur legend, moved along swiftly and to an appreciative audience, with plenty of laughs as King Arthur recruited his band of misfit knights.

At the end of the first act, applause was enthusiastic. Elise said, "They're good. Really good."

Mary Ann, with a chuckle, said, "I love that the king's squire is a female named Patsy. Great touch."

Following intermission, the second act was just as zany as the first, with lots of singing and lively choreography. When the show ended, the audience rose, applauding loudly. The cast began taking bows.

It was then that Mary Ann's cell phone vibrated. With a half-smile on her face she retrieved her phone from the pocket of her slacks.

A text message from Thaddeus Sinclair, editor and publisher of the *Camford Courier* weekly newspaper.

Mary Ann glanced at the message—and then, with a sharp intake of breath, moaned softly, "Oh, my God."

Elise stared at Mary Ann. "What is it?"

Her face stricken with pain, Mary Ann leaned in close and whispered, her voice not sounding like her own, "Becky from the library. Becky Thurston. Someone killed her."

CHAPTER TWO

Still grasping her phone, Mary Ann pushed her way through the crowd and headed to the auditorium's exit. People stopped to shake hands with cast members who were lined up in front of the stage.

Mary Ann kept mumbling "Excuse me . . . pardon me." She did briefly take the extended hand of one of the cast members, forced a smile, and said, "Enjoyed it very much. You're good."

She stepped out into the afternoon sunshine and headed for the driveway and Elise's car. Elise would be somewhere behind her, probably inside talking with the players. Mary Ann punched in her boss's cell phone number as she walked. One car waited for her as she darted across the driveway.

She listened to the rings . . . two, three . . . and on the fourth, it was answered.

"Sinclair."

"Thaddeus, oh my God. I got your message. That's awful. Unbelievable."

"A shock all right."

"Who?" She rested her hips against the locked door of Elise's car. Her voice choked, her words jumbled in her head. "I mean, who . . . do they know?" She forced a breath. "How was she . . . you know."

Thaddeus's voice was soft and controlled. "I'm at the police station now. The chief's in there talking to David Lynch, her boyfriend."

Mary Ann frowned. "The chief doesn't think . . . David

wouldn't hurt anyone. Not David."

"Police always look first at those closest to the victim. Spouses, boyfriends." He paused a moment. "And David was apparently the last one to be with her, and he's the one who found her and called 911."

Mary Ann pushed herself away from the car. "David wasn't the last one to see her. I'd say the killer was."

She could almost see Thaddeus get that half-smile of his. "I get your point." Then he added, "Just the same, Mary Ann—"

Mary Ann turned a bit to her right, watching Elise approach. As a reporter, she had to ask. At the same time, inquiring about details of her friend's death, felt vaguely ghoulish to her. "Thaddeus, how was she, you know, how was she killed?"

Again there was that pause on the other end of the line. Then Thaddeus said quietly, "She was beaten. Beaten to death."

"Oh, my God, that's awful." Mary Ann knew Elise stood watching her and hearing Mary Ann's end of the conversation. Again, she had to ask: "What with? What was she beaten with?"

Thaddeus, his voice even quieter, said, "I'll go over the details with you later." She heard him take a breath. "It was pretty brutal."

Then other voices sounded in the background.

Thaddeus said, "Chief Dalton's coming out now. I want to catch him."

They disconnected before Mary Ann could tell him that she would check again this evening, and certainly see him in the morning at the paper.

Mary Ann was aware that Elise kept studying her face.

"I'm so sorry," Elise said. "I know she was your friend, colleague at the library. I knew her, but just barely."

Mary Ann didn't say anything. She leaned back against Elise's car again. Her shoulders sagged. She shook her head, staring down at the pavement.

Elise touched Mary Ann's shoulder. Then clicked her key fob to unlock the doors. "We might as well go, Mary Ann."

Mary Ann nodded and turned to open the passenger door.

She slid into the seat and fumbled with the seat belt. She thought there ought to be tears in her eyes, but there weren't. She felt numb and empty.

Elise drove slowly out of the parking area, waited for a break in the traffic and then pulled into the center lane and eased into the eastbound light traffic. They were silent until Elise had made the left turn toward the Roanoke Sound. "We ought to get something to eat," Elise said.

"I'm not hungry," Mary Ann said, her voice dull, a monotone. She stared straight ahead.

"I know you're not, but you got to eat." Elise glanced at her and back at the road. "Even just a little something."

Mary Ann gave the slightest nod, barely any movement at all. She thought about Becky Thurston and the last time she'd seen her. It was at the Camford Courthouse Library of course. Not yesterday. Becky was off. It was the previous Saturday where Mary Ann conducted story hour for a small group of children. That was her part-time job, which she enjoyed very much. She recalled she had wondered yesterday why Becky was not at work. She was almost always there on Saturday.

They crested the apex of the Washington Baum Bridge. Elise said, "We could stop at the Black Pelican for a quick meal."

Mary Ann didn't answer right away. Then she mumbled, "Okay." After her half-hearted response, she felt a bit guilty. After all, Elise had sprung for their trip to see the play and she was upbeat about the performance. No matter how depressed Mary Ann was about Becky, there was no sense in bringing Elise down, too. Mary Ann echoed Elise's comment. "We've got to eat."

There was nothing Mary Ann could find out about Becky's killing at this point. Thaddeus would be there at the police station as long as anything was going on. She could call Thaddeus tonight, or wait until in the morning and get a complete fill-in from him at the newspaper.

They continued on the Bypass in silence for several miles.

The traffic was a little heavy. Still some tourists visiting, with drivers apparently unsure where they should turn.

At Kitty Hawk Road, Elise turned right and pulled into the Black Pelican parking area. She found a spot in the main section, facing the ocean. The restaurant had retained the front section of the old lifesaving station, which at the turn of the twentieth century was on the east side of the Beach Road. As the ocean encroached, the main structure was moved back from the eroding beach and now was on the west side of the road. In 1903, the lifesaving station served also as the telegraph office and it was from here, on December 17, 1903, that the Wright Brothers sent the telegram to their father in Dayton, Ohio, that they had made successful powered and controlled flights in their airplane.

Mary Ann and Elise climbed the wooden steps up to the main entrance. A young hostess approached them smiling, and Elise said they'd like to sit at the front on what most people called the porch, a long room enclosed with windows on the ocean side of the building, which had obviously been added to considerably over the years. Still, it had an antiquated look to it.

They passed the display case with enticing desserts, and Elise exhaled an appreciative sigh. After going around the large square U-shaped bar, the hostess took them to a table at the far end of the porch and said something about who would be their server. Mary Ann didn't catch the name and it didn't make much difference to her anyway.

The server, another young woman in knee-length shorts and a Black Pelican T-shirt, with a tattoo of a butterfly on her left forearm, took their drink order. Elise wanted iced tea and Mary Ann settled for ice water with lemon. They both glanced through the menus. Elise ordered the quesadilla with shrimp and Mary Ann asked for the personal-size aloha pizza.

When the waitress left with the orders, Elise said, "What the hell's an aloha pizza?"

"Well, sort of Hawaiian. It's got pineapple, ham and cheese," Mary Ann said.

"Whoever heard of such a pizza," Elise said.

Mary Ann managed the trace of a smile. "It's delicious."

Elise shook her head. She toyed with her napkin and flatware. Then she said, "I know you're not in the mood to think in terms of enjoyment, but the play was good, wasn't it?"

"Yes, it was," Mary Ann said. "They did a great job. All of them."

They were quiet again.

Mary Ann looked up at Elise. "I'll be covering this story about Becky." With a shake of her head, she said, "First time I've ever covered a murder story about a friend of mine."

Softly, Elise said, "I understand." Then, "But I know you and you'll do a professional job."

"Yep," Mary Ann said.

"You don't know any of the . . . the details yet, do you?" Elise used the unfolding of her napkin to apparently delay her next question. "Whether she was . . . raped or anything."

Mary Ann hadn't thought of that. Or hadn't wanted to. "No details yet. Only that Thaddeus said she was beaten and that it was brutal."

Elise made a face. "That's terrible. Really awful." She paused as the waitress approached with their food. "Suspects?"

Mary Ann shook her head. "No, not good ones."

With a smile, the waitress put down their food and said, "Enjoy."

Elise eyed Mary Ann's pizza. "Actually, that doesn't look too bad."

While she ate, Mary Ann thought about Becky Thurston and what she knew about her. Becky lived alone in a little house on the edge of town. Mary Ann felt a twinge of guilt. She really didn't know that much about Becky.

As if their thoughts were on the same wavelength, Elise said, "As a realtor, I know her house. Becky's house. Two bedrooms. Cute little place and fixed up nicely." Elise took a bit of her quesadilla. "Frankly, I wondered how she could afford it. You know, with her salary at the library."

"Oh, I expect her parents helped her. They lived in the Raleigh area before he retired. He must have had a top job of some sort at the Research Triangle. They retired down to Kitty Hawk." Then she added, "And from things she said from time to time, I think her mother came from a lot of money, too."

Elise nodded her head and chewed. "That would explain it." After a moment she asked, "What was she like at work?"

Mary Ann realized that the library was virtually the only place she saw Becky, and then mostly on the Saturdays Mary Ann had story hour for the children. Too, Becky was in her twenties and Mary Ann was forty-seven. Maybe she couldn't be expected to know her that well. "Nice," Mary Ann said. "She was nice. Well, maybe a little moody."

"Moody?"

"Yes. You know, real talkative some days and sort of depressed acting and quiet other days. And then, she could be sort of—I don't know—cross or agitated from time to time."

Elise had almost finished her quesadilla. Mary Ann's small pizza was only half eaten. "You think maybe she was on something? Making her, as you say, 'moody.'"

"Drugs? Oh, I don't think so." She thought for a moment. "I don't know, of course. Maybe she took something . . . but I don't think drugs. Not illegal stuff."

Elise shrugged.

They settled their bills and got ready to leave. Elise led the way as they headed past the bar, where a half-dozen drinkers were scattered about. The wooden floor inclined slightly at the edge of the bar and Mary Ann kept her eyes down, watching where she stepped.

Then she saw the tattoo on the right leg of a young man who drank a beer from the bottle. She glanced up at him. He had his head turned slightly, eyes on Elise.

Mary Ann recognized him. She looked at the tattoo again. Up close, she could appreciate the intricate artistry, but the image, a stylized skull with blue roses twining through its eye sockets, made her shiver.

As Mary Ann and Elise stepped outside in the late afternoon sun, Mary Ann said. "That man at the bar. He's the same one we saw when we left Belk's. Tattoo, ponytail."

Elise made that little shrug of hers as they headed down the steps. "It's a tiny little strip of sand, these Outer Banks."

She said it dismissively, as if this explained everything.

CHAPTER THREE

They arrived back in Camford Courthouse shortly after six. Elise drove Mary Ann to the two-story white frame house on Sycamore Street Mary Ann shared with her nineteen-year-old son Jerry. Mary Ann and her late husband Alan had bought the house, built in 1929 and renovated over the years, when they first moved from Connecticut to Camford Courthouse ten years ago. Alan had taken over a small insurance agency and they loved it here. Three years earlier, during a rehearsal of the romantic comedy *The Third Best Sport* at the Tracks Community Theater, with Alan in the lead, he suffered a massive heart attack and dropped dead on stage.

It was not until this past spring that Mary Ann ventured back into the theater, where Jerry was active in lighting and sound production.

Elise left the motor running on her Mustang but shifted into park. Mary Ann opened the passenger door. "You going to be okay?" Elise asked.

"Oh, yes, sure," Mary Ann said. "Jerry's still at work until seven tonight." A quick bob of her head. "I'm fine."

"I'll give you a ring tomorrow at the paper. See what you've found out."

"Thank you again, Elise, for the afternoon, shopping, play and everything."

"Don't forget your granny pajamas." Elise grinned.

"I've got them," Mary Ann said, clutching the Belk shopping bag, stepping out and closing the car door.

Elise waved and drove away.

Mary Ann mumbled to herself, but with a smile, "They're not granny pajamas." She started for the steps up to the front porch but stopped to pinch off several of the dead petunia blossoms in the concrete planters on each side of the steps. Her first two fingers and thumb felt sticky when she finished, and she rubbed them together, resisting her first impulse to wipe her fingers on her slacks.

Inside the hallway, she breathed in the familiar aroma of home. She had noticed years ago that everyone's house smelled different. She liked the comfortable scent of her own home. There was maybe the lingering homey scent of countless meals, a faint woodsy smell, and perhaps a hint of her own and that of son Jerry's fresh showers.

The living room was to her left, the dining room just beyond it. The stairs were close by on her right and she went upstairs to her bedroom in the front of the house. Jerry's bedroom was in the back. They shared a bath at the end of the hall upstairs. A half-bath had been added downstairs off the kitchen years earlier.

Mary Ann peeled off the slacks she had worn to the play, hung them in her closet and took off her top and hung that up carefully, too. She stood there a moment in the cotton panties and bra. Digging out a pair of baggy sweat pants, she put those on. She started to take her bra off, but decided against it when she slipped into a lightweight knit top with short sleeves.

Glancing at her watch, she went down to the kitchen and opened the refrigerator door, pondering. She probably ought to be prepared to fix something for Jerry when he came home from Food Lion at seven. Usually he snacked on something there from the deli and wasn't hungry when he came home. Just the same.

Jerry worked part-time at Food Lion because he had started his first year at College of the Albemarle in nearby Elizabeth City, planning to go there two years and then transfer to the University of North Carolina at Wilmington to major in film and theater production.

Mary Ann closed the refrigerator door, glanced at her watch again, and picked up the phone that hung against the kitchen wall. No one else she knew had a phone that hung on the wall. Sort of vintage. But she did, and she liked it. Punching in Thaddeus's cell number, she listened to the first ring, the second, and Thaddeus answered.

"I wanted to touch base again," Mary Ann said. "Hope this isn't a bad time."

"No, I'm back at the paper for a few minutes. Left the police station about twenty minutes ago. Hung around a long time." He sighed.

Mary Ann heard the familiar squeak of his desk chair as he leaned back. She could picture him sitting there, probably rubbing one palm across his curly—almost kinky—rust-colored hair, which he cut himself. It was touched now with a quite bit of gray. He would peer over the tops of his little round steel-framed John Lennon glasses, scribbling on a note pad with one of the many No. 1 pencils that cluttered his desk.

Mary Ann once described Thaddeus as a "rumpled skeptic," a phrase he had smiled at, and one he apparently felt was apropos. To Mary Ann, he looked more like what a newspaper reporter should look like than anyone she had ever met. Including wearing one of the oxford-weave button-down shirts he washed himself.

She was drawn to him; she knew that, but she tried—usually, and usually successfully—to ignore that pull that he had for her. Mary Ann sensed, too, that Thaddeus was attracted to her but, aside from a single dinner date shortly after she'd started working at the paper, refrained from any overt signs. At least she *hoped* that he had to refrain himself and that he really was maybe more than a little smitten with her. *Smitten? Did people ever even use that word anymore?*

Mary Ann was determined to keep her voice even, professional sounding. "Any further developments?"

"No, not really. Chief Dalton interrogated David Lynch, the

boyfriend, a long time. More than an hour and a half. But let him go. Told him not to leave town. Usual stuff cops tell so-called 'persons of interest.'"

"I can't . . . well, I can't picture David doing anything violent."

"Never can tell." Thaddeus paused, and Mary Ann heard his chair make that loud squeak again as he shifted position. "Whoever did it, did it thoroughly."

Mary Ann swallowed. "What do you mean?"

"She was beaten. Badly."

"Not, you know, stabbed or shot or anything?"

"No. Beaten." She pictured Thaddeus shaking his head. "Like it was personal."

"That's terrible, Thaddeus. Just horrible."

He cleared his throat. "I'm writing the basic story for this week's paper. I'll want you to do some sidebars and we'll go over those tomorrow."

"Okay," Mary Ann said.

There was another pause and then Thaddeus said, "You all right?"

"Yes. Stunned, I guess. Well, sad. Can't believe it." She took a breath. "But all right."

"See you in the morning," he said.

Mary Ann put the phone back in its wall cradle. She perched on the stool by the phone, staring off across the kitchen. She sighed and stood, knowing she had to think about some sort of light supper in case Jerry wanted to eat. She should eat something also; just a little something. The pizza at the Black Pelican had been a long time ago it seemed.

Shortly after seven, Jerry came home. He wore jeans and the Food Lion shirt and nametag pinned above the breast pocket. He gave his mother a little peck on the check and looked at her. "You okay?"

"That's what Thaddeus asked me a few minutes ago."

"He stop by?"

"On the phone," she said. "But yes, I'm okay"

"I figured you heard about Becky."

She nodded. Tilting her chin, she said, "You hungry?"

He shrugged. "Not really. I got something at the store." Then, "Oh, I ran one of the registers for a while today."

She managed a smile. "That's wonderful. Proud of you."

He glanced around the kitchen. "Cereal maybe. That'd be enough."

"Well, me too," Mary Ann said. "I had some pizza earlier."

"How was the play?"

"Wonderful. They did a great job." She took a breath and sighed. "It had just ended when Thaddeus texted me about Becky."

"Hard to believe," Jerry said, looking at her.

She got the cereal and milk. "I know," she said. She was determined to carry on and not give in to thinking too much about Becky. From the refrigerator she pulled out a plastic bag with four leftover biscuits. "I'll make some toasted cheese biscuits." She turned on the toaster oven.

They were quiet as they sat at the kitchen table eating. Mary Ann moved some of the cereal around in the bowl with the tip of her spoon.

Jerry took a small bite of one of the cheese biscuits, looking at his mother. "Thinking about Becky?"

Mary Ann didn't answer right away. Then she looked up at Jerry. "Well, it worries me, but I was thinking more about what I will write about her and about her killing than I was thinking about her . . . I mean her as a person, as a friend." With a little shake of her head, she said, "I was mentally writing my lead for a story, how I would do it." Then a short, self-deprecating shrug. "I've got to wonder what sort of person I've become if I think more about how I will write a story about her than I think *about* her."

"You're a reporter," Jerry said quietly.

Mary Ann sighed. "Yes, I guess I am."

CHAPTER FOUR

The next morning Mary Ann was showered and dressed early. By eight-thirty she was in her ancient Volvo station wagon and headed to the *Camford Courier* newspaper. Jerry had left shortly after seven for classes at the College of the Albemarle, or COA, as it was referred to. That summer he had bought a well-used Nissan pickup for commuting to school.

The newspaper was on Main Street in a white frame building with a wide wooden porch. Riggs Realty had a small office off the same porch, a few feet from the newspaper's front door. Mary Ann stepped inside the *Camford Courier* and smelled the familiar newsprint, ink, and printing supplies. She hadn't been in the paper since Friday and in just that short time the smells were like brand new to her. She breathed in and felt at home.

Ethel was already at her cluttered metal desk just inside the front door and raised her eyes at Mary Ann. As usual she did not smile, and today her expression was even more somber than usual. "Bad about Becky Thurston," Ethel said.

"Yes. Terrible," Mary Ann said.

Ethel went back to whatever she was doing. Mary Ann was never quite sure what that was. Thaddeus had inherited Ethel, who had been with the paper for at least two decades, and a couple of correspondents, when he left *The Washington Post* and bought the small weekly paper four years earlier, a dream he had had for years. As part of the package, a thriving print and copying shop was in the rear of the newspaper offices.

Mary Ann went straight back to Thaddeus's office. He was

at his desk and looked up at her over the tops of his glasses. He had a mug of coffee in front of him and had been reading copy. It was probably a story he had worked on earlier.

Muted greetings, and Mary Ann took the seat in front of his desk, her slim reporter's notebook in hand.

"Coffee?" he said.

She shook her head and then watched him take a sip of his coffee. She could smell the coffee. "Well, maybe so," she said and went to the new Keurig machine. Thaddeus had finally junked the older machine, which he was forever leaving turned on, stinking up the place with the odor of burned coffee.

Mary Ann got her coffee and came back to the chair in front of the desk while the Keurig ended the groaning it did when it finished dispensing a cup.

"Nothing really new," Thaddeus said. "I'm sorry about your friend, your colleague."

"The details, Thaddeus, about how she was killed. You said she was beaten and that it was brutal, and that you'd give me the details later." She held her chin up. She tried to make herself feel detached, like a reporter. She was conflicted, but she needed to know the details. As a reporter she needed to know.

Thaddeus put the copy he was editing to one side. He kept his fingers lightly on the coffee mug and looked at Mary Ann a moment or two before he said anything. "Beaten to death, as I said on the phone."

Mary Ann held her coffee mug tightly, her eyes cast down. She took a breath and a tentative sip of the coffee. She set the coffee on the edge of Thaddeus's desk. "Beaten with what?"

"All tentative, but it appears beaten with fists. Probably kicked as well." He kept his eyes on Mary Ann. "She likely hit her head on the edge of the coffee table at one point."

Mary Ann was determined to maintain a professional composure. She had her notebook open but hadn't written anything in it. She bit lightly on her lower lip and then she scribbled "beaten" in her notebook.

Thaddeus had remained motionless, his eyes still trained on

Mary Ann.

Mary Ann looked up. "How do you know all this, Thaddeus?" On Sundays, especially with the beautiful fall weather, Thaddeus would be out in his boat fishing the Pasquotank River. When would he have had time to learn all this?

As if reading her thoughts, Thaddeus said, "Police scanner. I was getting ready to go out when I heard a call for the rescue squad. I followed it up and arrived at her place the same time Chief Dalton got there." Thaddeus gave the barest hint of a smile for the first time. "Dalton tolerates me."

Mary Ann knew that Police Chief Tom Dalton more than "tolerated" Thaddeus. The chief trusted Thaddeus completely and had obvious respect for him, maybe even professional admiration.

"So you were there . . . right at the scene. In the beginning."

Thaddeus nodded.

"Was she . . . was she raped?"

"They don't know yet. But her clothes were mostly ripped off of her."

"Where is she? Where'd they take . . ." She hated to say it, but she said, ". . . the body?"

"Transferred to Greenville for a full autopsy. They did that yesterday afternoon." Thaddeus straightened in his chair. "Okay, we'll get more details as we go along, but first things first. I'm doing the basic story, telling as much as I can, and I'd like you to do a profile of her. I mean you knew her. You know people she knew. That sort of thing." He stared hard at Mary Ann. "You feel up to it?"

She tilted her chin up. "Yes."

"Good."

Mary Ann retrieved her coffee from the edge of the desk and made the initial movements as if rising from the chair.

Thaddeus held up a finger. "At ten o'clock Chief Dalton is holding a small press conference. Three or four reporters and a TV guy have called, starting yesterday. You and I will go."

Mary Ann nodded and rose. "I know you said the chief was

interviewing David Lynch yesterday." She shook her head. "I can't see him being, you know, violent or anything." She managed a tiny chuckle. "He's more the bookkeeper type than anything."

Thaddeus smiled at her. "Bookkeeper type or not, the young man has a black belt or some such in a type of martial arts that involves a combination of boxing and kick-boxing."

Mary Ann stood there holding her coffee cup, looking at Thaddeus.

"He's even a part-time instructor up in Chesapeake one evening a week," Thaddeus said.

This was something that Mary Ann didn't know about David. But she realized that he did look muscular and athletic. Could he have become enraged over something between them?

By nine-thirty that morning, the other reporter—Gene Paulson —a man about Mary's age who had been with the paper even before Thaddeus bought it, came into the small office he shared with Mary Ann. He said something about it being too bad about Becky Thurston, but Mary Ann only half-listened to him. He then mumbled that he would be covering the board meeting that night. Mary Ann managed a smile. She didn't want to be impolite, but she really did want to get back to her work. Although she never voiced it, she considered him rather lazy and not much of a reporter. Thaddeus appeared to tolerate him but never gave him any assignments that required digging or enthusiasm. She was relieved when he left.

Shortly before ten, Mary Ann took her notepad and went into Thaddeus's office. He stood behind his desk, picking up a pen and legal pad.

"Okay," he said. "Let's go."

The police station was just two blocks down Main Street. The building was another white frame structure that had recently been repainted. Two thriving shrubs were planted near the front steps. Black letters affixed to the front of the building proclaimed Camford Courthouse Police Department. Rather fancy looking.

Three cars were parked in front of the headquarters, along with a van with the lettering for a Norfolk television station. "Chief's drawing a crowd," Thaddeus said as he and Mary Ann approached the steps to the small porch at the entrance.

Thaddeus greeted the dispatcher who sat at a desk behind the Formica-topped counter. The dispatcher barely flicked a smile in return and pointed to the left. They entered the fair-sized room where Chief Dalton held briefings. A dozen or so folding metal chairs lined in front of a scarred brown wooden podium. Mary Ann and Thaddeus took seats near the back on the right.

Four reporters sat at the front. One was the newsman from the television station. His cameraman stood back with a shoulder-held camera so he could frame his reporter and the podium. The others were a young woman reporter representing the *Daily Advance* out of Elizabeth City; a male reporter from the Norfolk *Virginian-Pilot*; and a reporter from the weekly *Outer Banks Sentinel*.

Right at ten o'clock, Chief Dalton entered from a side door near the back of the briefing room. Accompanying him were two uniformed officers, a man and a woman. Chief Dalton conferred quietly with them as they approached the podium. Both officers were relatively new to the force. The woman, Lib Owens, mid-twenties, had short blonde hair pulled back in a small tight bun. She was petite and pretty. Mary Ann looked at her and consciously squared her own shoulders and tucked in her stomach.

Mary Ann had seen the other officer, Boyd Crocker, at her fitness center where he was a regular member. He was tall and broad-shouldered, and obviously spent time in the gym following a more rigorous workout than she did.

Neither of them smiled as they stood behind the chief and off to one side. Mary Ann wasn't at all sure why they were present unless it was to lend an air of formality to the press conference.

Chief Dalton, in his dark blue and gray uniform instead of his usual khaki pants and shirt, cleared his throat and thanked the reporters for coming.

"As all of you know by now, we've had a homicide here in the town this weekend. Becky Thurston, the victim, was found early Sunday morning at her home. Deceased." He paused a moment to glance at a small piece of paper he had laid on the podium. "The investigation is just underway, but we assume so far that she was killed sometime Saturday night."

The woman from the *Daily Advance* raised her hand and, without waiting for the chief to acknowledge her, blurted out, "How was she killed, Chief Dalton?"

The question caused Dalton to fumble with the little paper in front of him. He glanced back for an instant at Officer Boyd Crocker, who gave the barest nod of his head. "She was beaten," Dalton said, his words coming out a bit jumbled and hesitant.

"How was she beaten, Chief?" the woman asked. "Do you have the murder weapon?"

"Well, not specifically," the chief said.

The reporter from the *Virginian-Pilot* spoke out, "Sir, what do you mean by 'not specifically'?"

"We're still trying to determine some . . . some basic facts," Chief Dalton said. He was looking more and more uncomfortable.

The woman reporter again: "Was she sexually attacked? Raped?"

"We'll know more when we get the medical examiner's report, probably by tomorrow."

The TV reporter spoke out, using his on-camera voice, "Can you tell us whether, one, this was robbery, and if not, whether it was a crime of passion, and, two, do you have any suspects?"

"Well, not specifically, as far as suspects. And we don't know at this juncture whether robbery was involved. We are still inventorying her belongings to see whether anything is missing." He rubbed his palm across his forehead. "But back to suspects, we'll be talking with a number of people."

The woman reporter hardly allowed Dalton time to finish his sentence before she asked, "Who found her?"

"A friend of hers checked on her Sunday morning and called 911."

The woman was about to ask something else when the reporter for the *Outer Banks Sentinel* spoke up. "What about her parents? I'm sure you've been in touch with them down in Kitty Hawk . . ."

The chief appeared somewhat relieved with the question. "Yes, yes, of course. We contacted them immediately and they came up last evening and we went over everything we could with them. Naturally, they are very distraught. We've promised them that we will keep them apprised of everything as we move forward with the investigation . . . which, as I've said, is just underway."

Another question was about to come his way, but the chief held his palms toward the group and continued. "Yesterday we had the SBI lab personnel come and go over the scene very carefully. They will be giving us a full report. And we will probably have the report by tomorrow from the medical examiner. At that time, when those reports come in, I will be able to give more specifics."

There was a clamoring of half-articulated questions from the reporters, one voice falling over the top of another.

Dalton held his palms up again. "For now, that does it. Thank you all for coming."

Dalton and his two officers exited, amid one or two shouted questions as they slipped back through the side door.

As Mary Ann and Thaddeus left and started walking back to the paper, Mary Ann looked up at Thaddeus and said, "I don't believe we know any more than we did when we went there."

Thaddeus got that half-smile of his. Sounding like he was imitating the chief, he said, "Not specifically."

CHAPTER FIVE

When they got back to the newspaper, Mary Ann followed Thaddeus into his office.

She took the seat in front of his desk. He sat in his chair and looked at her. "Okay, Thaddeus," she said, "you went in Becky's house the same time the chief did. You said it was brutal and that her clothes were in . . . in disarray." She held her shoulders up, chin tilted. "I want to know how brutal, and whether you think she was raped, and was she nude or almost nude or what?" She tried to manage something of a smile. It didn't quite work. "And don't give me any of that 'not necessarily' business."

Thaddeus did give one of his half-smiles. "Being a reporter, huh?" He put both of his forearms on his desk. "Yes, it was brutal. There was quite a bit of blood. In the living room where her body was." He kept his eyes on Mary Ann. "As for her clothes, her blouse was ripped open. Her bra torn away exposing her breasts. The sweat pants she had on—more of calf-length slacks than sweat pants—were pulled down, along with her underwear. These clothing items were bunched around the ankles of her left leg. She was on her back. The right leg and stomach, her genital area, were bare."

Mary Ann tried to keep her expression blank. She wasn't completely successful.

Thaddeus said, "As for rape, this is not a 'not necessarily' statement, but the medical examiner will try to make a determination."

He glanced at his desktop and then back to Mary Ann. "There was no evidence of forced entry into the house. The front door was unlocked and partly open. Her boyfriend, David Lynch, may have left the door partly open when he went there that morning and found her."

Mary Ann was quiet for a moment, framing her words in her mind. "Becky and David were very close and had been going together for several months at least. Maybe a year. If they were as close as they appeared to be, I don't see why he would have, you know, ripped her clothes and all. Not trying to say anything disrespectful, but I don't believe he would have, well, would have had to."

Thaddeus said, "Except that he admitted to the chief that he and Becky had argued earlier Saturday night and he had left. He indicated he was going back that morning to apologize for blowing up—when he found her."

"But from what you say, it looked like somebody was raping her . . ."

"Or trying to make it look like she was raped," Thaddeus said.

Mary Ann was silent. Then, "Anybody else the chief is looking at?"

"Not necessarily."

She gave him a look.

He hunched a slight shrug. "Not trying to make light of it. But that's the truth. There is no one else the chief has been able to come up with to question. Her house is pretty much separated from her neighbors, but he's sent officers to interview neighbors, see if they saw or heard anything unusual that night." He toyed with one his pencils. "Nothing so far."

Mary Ann sighed. "Guess I'd better get on that profile." She started to rise.

Thaddeus said, "In the bathroom, medicine cabinet was open. The usual stuff in there, all thrown around. There were no prescription medications there."

"Maybe she didn't have any," Mary Ann said. She shook

her head. "I doubt that, though, because I know she had been to see doctors about her lower back."

"Also, the drawer in her bedside table was pulled out, contents dumped on the bed. Nothing much more than you would expect. It was as if someone was looking for something." He twirled the pencil in his fingers. "There was no blood in the bedroom. Probably searched after she was dead."

Mary Ann settled back in her chair, her brow furrowed. "Looking for something to steal? Medicines? Drugs?"

"Don't know. Could be something to steal." He raised one eyebrow. "Could be trying to get rid of something. Hide it. But it's certainly part of the puzzle."

Mary Ann rose again, still frowning, thinking. "Well, Becky was really moody, especially lately. She'd be up one day—one hour—and then down the next. I confess that I sort of, you know, wondered . . ."

Thaddeus looked over the top of those little glasses. "You think she was taking anything? Any drugs?"

"Oh, I don't know," Mary Ann said. "I just thought, probably something for her back."

Thaddeus nodded. "Yet—at least when we looked, as I said —there were no prescription medications at her house." He paused a beat or two. Then he added, "You know which doctor she went to?"

"No, but I can find out," she said.

He nodded. "For now, you'd better get on that profile. Talk with the usual people. Who were her friends in high school in Kitty Hawk, college friends, people at the library? We want a word picture of her."

"I know," she said. "And I want to know who killed her."

"So do I," he said.

Back at her desk, Mary Ann plopped in her chair. Gene Paulson said something to her about how the press conference went, and she mumbled a response, and then, trying to be a bit more polite, turned her head to speak to him before getting to work.

She scribbled some names on a legal pad, starting with Sue Wilson, the head librarian, and another coworker. Mary Ann remembered one name of a high school friend of Becky's whom she had mentioned from time to time. She would try her and once she got started, other names would surface.

She worked on interviewing acquaintances of Becky's for an hour before she started writing anything. It was interesting to her but the friends from earlier years talked about how calm and even-tempered Becky was. She didn't get a picture of a moodier, more up and down emotional nature until current friends and coworkers. She puzzled over how to handle that in the story; then figured that was something she would keep more or less to herself for the time being, except in talking with Thaddeus, or mentioning to Elise.

Glancing at the round wall clock over her desk, she realized it was time for lunch—a late lunch. Her stomach reminded her of that fact also. As if on cue, Thaddeus appeared at her door and said, "Want to grab a bite to eat?"

"Yes. Time slipped up on me."

Gene Paulson had shuffled out for lunch forty-five minutes earlier, and Ethel had already eaten something brought from home. Thaddeus told Ethel that he and Mary Ann would be back in about half an hour or so. Ethel nodded.

Walking side-by-side, Mary Ann and Thaddeus took the two blocks down Main Street, past the police station, and jaywalked to the left for the short block to Scarborough Street and Bunny's Restaurant. The only words exchanged as they walked occurred when they passed the police station. Thaddeus said, "We may stop back there and see if Chief Dalton has heard anything on the autopsy."

Mary Ann looked up at Thaddeus and said, "Okay. Fine."

They entered Bunny's and were greeted with a big smile by Bunny Metcalf herself. She was in her fifties and obviously enjoyed partaking of quite a bit of her own cooking. She showed them to a table about two-thirds of the way back.

At one time the red brick building had housed a locally

owned hardware store. But it went out of business when larger
homebuilding stores came to the area. Bunny's still kept the feel
of another generation. The floors were wide wooden planks,
oiled and sanded over the years. Wooden planters with thriving
flowing ferns added an airy tone to the interior. Plenty of lighting, some from rustic wooden chandeliers. Bunny's was the favorite of the courthouse crowd and business people, especially
for lunch.

Today the lunch crowd had thinned a bit. When Mary Ann
and Thaddeus took seats, a young waitress in a Bunny's T-shirt
and tight jeans came to their table and asked about drinks. Her
sandy colored hair was short and brushed back.

"Just water," Thaddeus said.

Mary Ann studied the menu, even though she knew what
she would order. "Same," she said with a quick smile at the
waitress.

When the waitress returned with ice water in glasses bead-
ed with moisture, Thaddeus said they were ready to order.

The waitress smiled at Thaddeus. "You want your usual?"

"Sure," he said.

"Reuben on rye with Thousand Island on the side. Plenty of
sauerkraut."

"You got it," he said.

She turned to Mary Ann, her smile not quite as bright.

"Your chef salad," Mary Ann said.

"Dressing?"

"Ranch." Another quick smile from Mary Ann. "On the side."

The waitress nodded and scurried away to place their orders.

Mary Ann raised her eyebrows, a little twist of her head.
"We're getting to be creatures of habit."

Thaddeus nodded. He seemed to be studying an invisible
spot on the table. When he didn't say anything for a minute or
more, Mary Ann said, "Becky Thurston story?"

"Yeah." He was quiet again. Then he looked up at Mary
Ann. "It didn't appear that anything was stolen from her house.

I mean there was thirty-seven dollars still in her wallet and her purse was emptied out. Wallet was lying right beside the things that were in her purse. Usual things, I guess. Lip balm, a little compact. The medicine cabinet gone through." He frowned. "But no prescriptions of any kind. Practically everyone has some prescription bottles around. A few anyway."

Mary Ann said, "I'll check with her doctor, as soon as I find out which one. Maybe check with one or two of the pharmacists."

The waitress brought Thaddeus's sandwich and Mary Ann's chef salad. Three little packets of saltine crackers were on the plate with the salad and the dressing in a tiny pitcher to the side.

"Enjoy," the waitress said and went quickly to another table where clothing storeowner Dewey Womble had just taken a seat. But he got up before he had hardly settled and stepped over to their table to speak to Thaddeus. "Got a murder story to write about this week. The young woman who was raped and killed?"

"Hello, Dewey," Thaddeus said. "Well, it's certainly a homicide but we don't know that she was raped."

Dewey Womble shrugged. "Heard she was. Raped."

"Autopsy is being performed," Thaddeus said.

Womble stood there a beat. He glanced at Mary Ann. "Didn't mean to interrupt your lunch." He smiled weakly, bobbed his head and went back to his table, where the waitress appeared, notepad in hand.

Silently, Mary Ann fumed. *As soon as anyone learns of a woman being murdered, first thing they ask about is whether she was raped. Like it's almost to be expected.*

Thaddeus dipped one corner of his sandwich in the container of Thousand Island dressing and took a bite. Chewing, he said, "Maybe prescription drugs is what the killer was looking for, stealing."

Mary Ann poured a thin stream of ranch dressing on her salad and pushed some of the ingredients, cheese and julienned

ham and turkey, around with her fork to take advantage of the
dressing. Before taking a forkful of salad that was poised over
her plate, she trained her eyes toward Thaddeus but was not
really focused on him. It was if she stared at a thought beyond
him. "Or maybe the killer didn't want prescriptions to be
found." There was the tiniest frown.

Thaddeus cocked his head at her. "Why?"

Mary Ann shrugged, brought the fork close to her mouth. "I
don't know. I was just trying to look at it from the other end.
Upside down."

Thaddeus said, "Always a good reporter's technique. Take
the obvious and then turn it around."

"Habit of mine," Mary Ann said and popped the forkful of
salad in her mouth. She chewed away, trying to be a little deli-
cate.

While they ate, Thaddeus outlined what he'd like for Mary
Ann to concentrate on in doing a profile of Becky Thurston. He
wanted her not only to talk to Becky's colleagues at the library
and friends she might have, but to talk with her boyfriend David
Lynch, not as a suspect but as someone who was close to her.
At some point, Thaddeus said he'd like for Mary Ann to go
down to Kitty Hawk and talk with her parents and former
friends there. "This is going to be an ongoing story, I do believe," Thaddeus said. "You'll be doing more than one or two
stories . . . and I think I will be too."

Mary Ann said, "It's going to be with us a while?"

"I'm afraid so," Thaddeus said.

They finished eating mostly in silence. Then Thaddeus
signaled the waitress for the check. Mary Ann brought out her
wallet. He shook his head. "Working lunch. On me."

"Seems you're always feeding me," Mary Ann said.

"You don't eat that much."

Involuntarily, she sucked her stomach in. "That was a wonderful meal we had at the Colington Café down at the Outer
Banks. You know, when I first came with the paper full time. I
can see why it is one of your favorites. It was fun."

"We'll do it again," he said, looking straight into her eyes.

After the bill was settled, Thaddeus rose. "Let's go see Chief Dalton. Maybe he's heard something from Greenville on the autopsy."

CHAPTER SIX

They spoke to Bunny on the way out and said they enjoyed their meals. The fall weather was balmy and bright. The weather was forecast to remain pleasant for the next several days, even though there was a hurricane churning off islands in the Caribbean that all of those along the Outer Banks and coastal areas were keeping an eye on.

Mary Ann glanced at her watch. Five minutes after two. They headed to police headquarters.

They mounted the three steps to the front porch of the white frame station. "We need to get some fresh paint on our front," Thaddeus said.

The dispatcher, a fortyish woman with very short hair and a nametag that said Chaney, sat behind the counter. She raised her eyebrows questioningly at Thaddeus and Mary Ann.

"We'd like to see the chief," Thaddeus said.

Without responding, the woman picked up the telephone handset, punched one number and said, "Mr. Sinclair is here to see you." She listened. Then to Thaddeus she said, "You all can go on back."

"Thanks, Officer Chaney," Thaddeus said.

The dispatcher nodded and almost smiled.

Mary Ann followed Thaddeus around the counter and down the short hallway to Chief Dalton's office. His door was partly open and two uniformed officers stood in front of his desk. Mary Ann recognized them—the young woman officer, Lib Owens, and the husky Boyd Crocker, both of whom were with the chief at the press conference. They glanced over their shoulders at Mary Ann and Thaddeus. They appeared ready to leave.

"Come on in," Dalton said.

"Didn't mean to interrupt you," Thaddeus said.

"No problem. Just going over some things with officers Owens and Crocker."

With slight nods to Thaddeus and Mary Ann, the two officers left.

The chief tilted his head at the two chairs in front of his desk. "Have a seat." With a trace of a smile, Dalton said, "Your timing's good." One eyebrow raised with mock questioning, he said, "You got an 'in' with the medical examiner's office?"

"Wish I did," Thaddeus said.

". . . 'Cause I just got a preliminary autopsy report not twenty minutes ago. Going over it a bit with Crocker and Owens."

"That was quick," Thaddeus said.

Mary Ann sat silently, shoulders erect, back straight.

"They must've put in overtime Sunday." The chief shook his head. "Guess they got the budget for it."

Thaddeus and Mary Ann waited expectantly. Thaddeus leaned forward. "Well . . . ?"

Dalton offered a weak smile. "Sorry. I was just thinking about budgets." He picked up three sheets of paper that apparently had been either faxed to him or sent electronically and he had printed out.

"Couple of surprises here, I guess." He heaved out a sigh, his lips and cheeks puffing out. Worry lines creased his forehead and around his eyes. He looked tired, older than his fifty-something years.

"No surprise about how she was killed," Dalton said. "Severe beating. Lots of internal damage. Busted spleen. Ruptured this, ruptured that. Busted jaw, nose, cheekbones. Some of the medical terms I gotta look up. But we got the picture. That wound on the back of her head was what they termed superficial. But that's where most all of that blood came from."

The image of a beaten and bloody Becky Thurston was in such stark contrast to the alive and sometimes-lively young woman that Mary Ann could hardly take it in. She could feel the emotional response down in her stomach. It made her feel sick.

In the lull when Dalton finished, Thaddeus said, "The couple of surprises?"

Dalton held the first sheet, studying it again. "Yeah. First off, she had some drugs in her. Opioids. Pain killers. Prescription stuff probably. Maybe something else, like an amphetamine, stimulant."

He shook his head. "And two, there was no evidence of rape . . ." He glanced briefly at Mary Ann as if he were concerned about couching his language in such a fashion as to not offend her.

Thaddeus apparently sensed this and spoke up. "Mary Ann is a reporter. She's heard all these details before. So . . ."

The chief nodded. "There was no bruising around her . . . her genital area, and no semen in her or on her." He put the paper down. "Of course, that doesn't mean she wasn't, you know, sexually active." He seemed to be thinking of something. "Maybe a condom involved. But no lubricant found. So probably not."

Questions bounced around in Mary Ann's head. She wanted to blurt them out, but declined, figuring she'd talk to Thaddeus about them later. Why were Becky's clothes half off of her? Why were there no prescription drugs there, and where had she been getting them?

"You going back over to the scene?" It had been silent for close to a minute before Thaddeus spoke up.

"Matter of fact I am," Dalton said. "Want to take another real close look around. The forensic guys have finished. Nothing startling there."

Mary Ann couldn't keep quiet any longer. "Pardon me, Chief, but as you know I worked with Becky most Saturdays and she complained about lower back pain." Mary Ann moistened her lower lip with the tip of her tongue. "She went to at least two or more doctors about the pain." She hesitated a beat because she realized she didn't want to be saying anything that reflected poorly on her now dead friend and former colleague. "Becky complained to me that the doctors didn't seem to know . . . weren't able to give her much relief."

Mary Ann sat straight and still. She resisted glancing at Thaddeus to see whether he approved of her speaking out. She kept her eyes on the chief.

Chief Dalton nodded slowly, his gaze on Mary Ann. "Do you know the names of these doctors?" His tone was level, penetrating. A cop's voice, Mary Ann thought.

"One was here in town. At least one other one was down on the Outer Banks. I don't know any names . . . not yet."

Thaddeus spoke up. "I'd assume that's where she got the pain medication." Thaddeus tilted forward slightly as if he wanted to be more personal in what he was saying to Dalton. "Now, Chief, I don't want to overstep my role as a reporter and . . ." He gave a short chuckle. ". . . and step on your toes in the process, but you could surely check pharmacies here in town, maybe the Outer Banks, see what she was getting. And of course, talk with the doctors, starting with those here in town."

Chief Dalton rubbed his palm over his forehead and across his thinning hair as if he were in pain. "No, I don't think you're overstepping anything, Thaddeus." He sighed again and shook his head. "Naw, I appreciate the suggestions. Really do."

Thaddeus continued, his voice soft. "And it was strange that we didn't find any prescription drugs at Becky Thurston's house. Not in her medicine cabinet, bedside table, or purse."

"Yeah . . ." Dalton said. "Just the usual female stuff there." He glanced quickly at Mary Ann. "No sexist remark meant there, Mary Ann." Then to Thaddeus: "At the time I didn't pay much attention to the fact that no prescription medications were there. But now, with the autopsy report . . ."

"The killer steal them?" Thaddeus said. "That what this is all about?"

Dalton sank back in his chair, as if deflated. "I don't know,

Thaddeus. I don't know a damn thing. I mean, I'm a good cop. I
really am. But tell the truth, I'm not an investigator. Not a homicide investigator." A wry, self-deprecating smile played briefly
on his face. "Hell, you've had more investigative experience
probably than I have. Didn't you cover crime up in Boston?"

"As a young reporter I spent a few years on the police beat
there. Then did investigative reporting at *The Washington Post*.
But I'm not a homicide investigator either. I'm sure you've
thought about whether to call for help from the state folks, the
SBI. There's an agent over near Elizabeth City."

"Yeah, I've thought about it. Figured we'd give it a shot
here in the department first . . ." His voice trailed off and then
he sat up straighter as if he was determined to have more re-
solve. "And let's start by going over the scene one more time.
See if something turns up there, now that we know a bit more
about her."

"Good idea," Thaddeus said. "You don't mind if we tag
along, do you?"

Dalton answered so quickly that Mary Ann recognized that
he had already considered it. "No, don't mind at all." He chuckled and eased himself out of his chair. "Maybe you two will
see something we've missed."

It was unusual for any police officer to be so agreeable to
having a couple of reporters accompany him. But this was a
small town, she reasoned, and Dalton obviously had a lot of respect for Thaddeus, and had come to trust him completely, even
more so than he had just a few months earlier on another case.
And since Thaddeus would be bringing her along, this gave her
a mantle of acceptance.

Too, she really did want to go to the scene, to Becky's
place—knowing full well she had disturbingly mixed and stirring emotions about being right there where Becky was killed.

CHAPTER SEVEN

Mary Ann and Thaddeus walked quickly back to the newspaper. Chief Dalton said he would come by there in about five minutes and they would drive in separate vehicles to Becky Thurston's house.

Mary Ann took long steps to keep up with Thaddeus. He glanced down at her. "You going to be all right going over to the scene?"

Mary Ann had been thinking about it. "Yes," she said. "Yes. I'm a reporter, remember?"

He smiled. "Okay."

When they got back to the newspaper's parking lot, Mary Ann hiked herself up into Thaddeus's truck by holding on to the bar inside the passenger door.

"Agile," Thaddeus said, as they buckled up.

Within a minute Chief Dalton swung by the newspaper and they followed him west out of the main part of town. They turned down a narrow road, then made another left onto an even smaller road. Becky Thurston's long gravel driveway lay before them. The sagging yellow and black crime scene tape stretched across the front of the small stucco house. There was no front porch to speak of, just two steps up to a tiny brick portico.

They ducked under the crime scene tape and Chief Dalton retrieved a key from his side pocket, unlocking the front door. Then he stopped and reached into his jacket and brought out blue latex gloves. "We'd better put these on," he said. "Not really necessary at this stage, but want to follow protocol."

Mary Ann took a pair of the gloves and slipped them on. She held one hand to her nose and sniffed. They had a peculiar smell, almost a rubbery odor. First time she had ever had latex gloves on. She had seen nurses and doctors wear them, of course, and she'd wondered what they would smell like, how they would feel.

Mary Ann's heart beat faster and her breathing was shallow. She forced herself to take a deep, lung-filling breath before they stepped inside.

"The door was not locked when we responded," Dalton said.

"I remember," Thaddeus said. "No evidence of forced entry."

"Yeah, that's one of the first things we noted."

Thaddeus said, "There was no real first responder since you and I and one of your officers and EMS personnel arrived at just about the same time."

"Yeah, except for her boyfriend, David Lynch, who phoned it in."

The three of them stepped inside, Mary Ann close behind Thaddeus and the chief. The air was stuffy. And was that death she smelled? She was conscious of Thaddeus giving her a quick glance. She kept her chin up, shoulders squared.

"Leaving the door open," Dalton said. "Get some air in here."

So it's not just me, Mary Ann thought.

After only a few steps beyond the front door, the tiny living room was off to the left. Obvious to Mary Ann, this was where the struggle took place. One small chair was overturned. The coffee table was cockeyed. One table lamp had been knocked to the floor, its shade mashed in the process.

Bloodstains had spattered the corner of the coffee table and a circle of brown blood pooled on the beige carpet. But there was not as much blood as Mary Ann had expected—or feared. Not quite as gruesome. Her eyes were drawn back to the dried blood in the center of the carpet. This had to be where Becky had ended up. Maybe it was the old blood she smelled. She turned her head. Her breathing was shallow again, and she kept it that way.

"We got pictures of all this," Dalton said. "Before she was moved."

The opened purse was on the sofa. Contents of the purse were dumped on the cushions. Mary Ann followed Thaddeus to the sofa and peered at the contents. Nothing more than she would have suspected. The wallet lay to one side.

"Thirty-seven dollars still in her wallet," Dalton said.

Mary Ann nodded. Thaddeus had already told her that.

"Not robbery . . . at least not robbery in the usual sense," Dalton said.

"But he was obviously looking for something," Thaddeus said.

For the first time, Mary Ann spoke, her voice a bit unsteady: "And I'd say he found it since you didn't find any prescription medications."

Both Thaddeus and Dalton looked at her and nodded agreements. Mary Ann sensed that Thaddeus was proud of her.

Mary Ann glanced again around the room, the other furnishings, and then the walls. There were three pictures on the wall. All three were of birds; one appeared to be an enlarged photograph of birds settling in a marsh, probably taken down at Pea Island. Also, knocked over on the coffee table was a beautiful crystal figurine about eight inches tall of a bird in flight. She had heard Becky mention several times about her love of birds.

"I thought she had a live bird in a cage here," Mary Ann said.

"No bird here," Dalton said.

Mary Ann nodded. That was several months ago when Becky had said something about a pet bird, and maybe the bird died.

They took a quick look in the kitchen. A couple of plates, three pieces of flatware, and a glass had been rinsed and set in the sink. Two potted houseplants sat near the window over the sink, where they caught the afternoon sun. The plants were wilted, and Mary Ann had to resist the urge to water them.

"We'll check the bathroom," Dalton said. Two doors were in the bathroom so that it could be entered either from the bedroom or the short hall.

The medicine cabinet was still open. Tylenol, a nose spray, a few other over-the-counter items. No prescription meds. Mary Ann opened the small closet in the bathroom. Towels neatly rolled, extra bathroom tissue, a small box of tampons on the second shelf.

Mary Ann said, "No contraceptives . . . birth control pills . . . devices." She glanced at Dalton. "Interesting. If she was supposed to be sexually active."

Dalton acknowledged her observation with a quick, small nod.

Mary Ann realized she'd gotten used to the smell in the house. *Strange how quickly a thing like that could start to seem normal. You get used to it, don't smell it any longer—even pleasant odors—and then when you come back it is there anew.*

They went to Becky's bedroom. Over the bed there was a large, framed picture of three pelicans skimming low over the ocean. A beautiful photograph, shot, it appeared, in the late afternoon, the clouds golden and reflecting on the waves.

The drawer in the bedside table was open. A small red leatherette covered New Testament. Purse-size box of tissues, a Vicks inhaler. Four library books stacked atop a bookcase. Mary Ann glanced at titles. *The Girl on the Train, A Gentleman in Moscow*, a couple of romances. None was overdue.

Mary Ann said, "I can turn these in at the library."

Chief Dalton hesitated a moment. "Naw, let's leave everything here for now. Day or so we'll make sure we're through with it as a crime scene."

"I guess her parents will see to closing up the house?" Thaddeus said.

"Yeah," Dalton said, shaking his head. "I know they'll hate

that task."

Mary Ann glanced once more around the bedroom. *This was Becky's home, where she slept.* Those thoughts ran through her head. But Mary Ann was surprised that she felt detached here at Becky's house. It was as if she had clicked a little switch upon entering the house that permitted her to remain an observer, a reporter gathering impressions, making mental notes about how to write the scene. She felt removed from anything personal, anything overly emotional.

That is, until she opened the closet door in Becky's bedroom.

Immediately Mary Ann smelled the faint light-floral scent of Becky. She recognized some of the clothes. Shoes were lined neatly on the floor of the closet and a cotton robe hung on the back of the door. *She'll never, ever be wearing any of these again.* Suddenly Mary Ann felt a flush of heat in her throat and she fought back scalding tears. She tried to control her breathing, and she bit down on her lower lip. She stood there with her hand on the closet doorknob. She forced her gaze away from Becky's clothes. She wanted to step back from the lingering light-floral scent, but for a moment she couldn't.

Mary Ann gave her head the slightest shake. Her neck felt stiff. She gently pushed the closet door shut.

She was aware that Thaddeus watched her.

He lightly touched her shoulder but remained silent.

Dalton had moved from the bedroom back to the living room. "Visiting here doesn't tell us a whole lot we don't already know, does it?" Dalton said.

Mary Ann and Thaddeus followed Dalton into the living room. Thaddeus spoke, his voice sounding loud in the silence of the house. "Well, it does tell us something. The killer was looking for something. Maybe he found it. We don't know for sure."

Mary Ann took a deep breath. She was determined to gain control of her sadness, to assume her role as a reporter. Her chin up, she said, "What about her clothes? I mean that they were just about off of her when you all got here, Mr. Sinclair said."

Mary Ann could see Thaddeus peering down at her over the tops of his little round glasses.

"I don't know," Dalton said. "Maybe he was getting ready to, you know, rape her. Maybe something scared him away."

Mary Ann felt bolder. "Well, I kind of doubt anything scared him away. It looks like he searched the bathroom and bedroom after she was . . . after she was killed."

Dalton mulled that over. Tentatively, he said, "Yeah . . ." and his voice trailed off.

"Maybe he wanted it to look like rape was the motive," Mary Ann said.

Dalton tilted his head questioningly.

"Possible," Thaddeus said. "Or maybe he was tearing off her clothes, she struggled, he beat her some more . . . then realized he'd killed her . . . and stopped."

Mary Ann thought about the comment that had been made earlier that perhaps a condom had been used. *No evidence of forced rape, but just maybe it wasn't forced at all in the beginning. If that was the case, does it point more to Becky's boyfriend?* She decided not to say anything further.

The three of them stepped out front onto the low brick steps. Dalton locked the front door and slipped the key into his pocket. They peeled off the latex gloves. Dalton offered to take them, dispose of them.

Mary Ann looked around. The nearest house was at least two hundred yards away. A few other houses were scattered about. "She was isolated here," Mary Ann said.

"Yeah," Dalton said, "and Officer Boyd Crocker checked with neighbors. No one saw anything unusual." He went to his cruiser, opened the driver's side door and eased his bulk inside.

"Thanks for letting us tag along, Chief," Thaddeus said.

Dalton sat there a moment, mulling something over. "Gotta talk with young David Lynch some more."

Thaddeus put one hand on top of the opened doorframe. "You really suspect him?"

"Hell, he's the only thing I've got right now."

Thaddeus nodded.

Dalton pulled his door closed, window down. "Probably be some more reporters' calls when I get back to headquarters." He shook his head and started the engine.

Mary Ann and Thaddeus went to his truck and Mary Ann swung herself up onto the passenger seat. They were silent as Thaddeus turned on the ignition. The pickup truck's engine made a low rumble as it came to life.

Mary Ann stared straight ahead. "Such a shame. A young life cut so short."

Thaddeus glanced over at her as he drove away from the house. "That's the title of the piece I want you to write for next week's edition: 'A Young Life Cut So Short.' Okay? That's the theme."

Mary Ann nodded, and thought about Becky Thurston.

CHAPTER EIGHT

The late afternoon was warm and golden when Thaddeus and Mary Ann pulled up to park his pickup at the newspaper. Getting out of the truck was easier for Mary Ann than getting in it.

They opened the front door of the newspaper office and Ethel spoke to them. "You got an obit here." She handed Thaddeus a sheet of paper. "From Phillip Mastik." Ethel raised her eyebrows as if she couldn't believe it. "Funeral for Ms. Thurston will be at his place. Not Baker's."

"Becky liked Phillip," Mary Ann said softly.

Ethel shrugged.

Baker's Funeral Home was the leading facility in Camford Courthouse, and Phillip Mastik's Eternal Rest ran a distant second.

Thaddeus scanned the obituary notice. "Saturday morning at ten," he said.

"I'll check with Sue at the library. But I expect it'll be closed for the funeral," Mary Ann said.

Thaddeus said to Mary Ann: "No children's story hour this week." It was as much of a question as a statement.

"Surely not," Mary Ann said. "Frankly, don't think I'd feel up to it anyway."

The two of them continued back to Thaddeus's office. Mary Ann stopped a few feet inside the door.

Thaddeus went behind his desk. Before he sat down he studied Mary Ann over the tops of his glasses. "You might as well call it a day," he said. "Start on that profile tomorrow."

She nodded, still standing there as if she couldn't make up her mind about something. "Well, I hope it's not too soon to talk with her parents . . . to go down to Kitty Hawk and visit them."

"Should be okay. Call them this afternoon or tomorrow."

Mary Ann turned to leave. "I'll start with Sue and others at the library, and then maybe see Mr. and Mrs. Thurston later in the week."

Thaddeus took his seat and picked up the copy he'd been working on.

As if an afterthought, he extended the obituary notice across his desk. "Might as well handle this before you leave." He looked at her again. "Then go on home."

She took the obit, paused a moment, the fingers of one hand touching lightly on the edge of Thaddeus's desk. "You think . . . you think I'm going to find out things about Becky that . . . that I'd rather not know?"

Thaddeus was silent. He looked down at his desk and then back up at Mary Ann. "You might," he said. His voice was quiet. "You just might."

At home, Mary Ann felt, as she described it to herself, "at loose ends." She went into the kitchen first and thought about supper, what she would have. It was only a few minutes after five and Jerry would be home any minute. She wasn't hungry, but she had to fix something. She put her cotton bag on the kitchen table. She used the bag as more or less a purse that carried her wallet, notepad, pens, and other items. It amounted to her all-in-one briefcase. She opened the refrigerator, peered inside; then closed it, picked up her bag and went upstairs to her bedroom to change clothes. She would decide on supper when she came back downstairs.

She slipped out of her slacks and blouse, hung them up, and retrieved a comfortable pair of sweats from the hook on the back of the closet door. Standing there at her closet, she thought again about Becky's clothes. The memory of that faint floral scent came back to her so strongly she could almost smell it. The terribly sad realization that Becky would never wear those clothes again assailed her anew. And it was the shoes, too. Just seeing those neatly lined up shoes that would never feel the heat of Becky's feet was unbearable, more so maybe than the clothes.

Mary Ann steeled herself against tears, took a deep breath, and stepped out of the closet, closed the door. She opened a drawer in the bureau to pull out a pullover shirt. When she opened the drawer, she saw her new pajamas, still wrapped in tissue. Buying the new pajamas seemed like something that had happened a long, long time ago.

She heard Jerry pull up in the driveway and park behind her Volvo. She went downstairs to greet her son, determined to wear a smile. Her chin held high, she gave him a peck on his cheek as he came in the door.

"Didn't expect you home yet," Jerry said.

"Been a long day. Thaddeus told me to go on home."

"Yeah, he wants to look after his ace reporter," Jerry said with that lilt of a tease in his voice. They started back to the kitchen, and he tossed over his shoulder, "That, and he's sort of sweet on you anyway."

"He's my boss, that's all," Mary Ann said. But she smiled and tried to sound stern. It was a tease that had been going on since Mary Ann started working again at the paper. When she and Alan had moved to Camford Courthouse from Connecticut—what was it, now almost six years ago?—she had worked briefly at the paper, a reporting career she had back in Connecticut, and then decided to stay home at Alan's urging. After he died, she had taken to babysitting at their home and working on Saturdays at the library, where, among other things, she'd stepped into her current role in charge of children's story hour. It was this past spring that she started again at the *Camford Courier*.

"School okay today?" Mary Ann asked.

"Fine. Just one class tomorrow. So I'll work at Food Lion from three to ten."

"Hungry?" Mary Ann said, looking again in the refrigerator.

"Not very." He stood so he could look in the refrigerator also. "Heck, soup and sandwich suits me."

Mary Ann nodded. "Me too. But I'll fix a couple of salads also."

They ate at the kitchen table. Jerry poured himself a glass of sweet iced tea. Mary Ann stuck with water.

Jerry took a bite of his ham and cheese sandwich. He chewed slowly and watched his mother. "How did it go today? I mean about the murder story."

Mary Ann took her time. "Thaddeus is doing the main story." She was aware that the two little lines of concern were there between her eyebrows. "I have a hard time, though, thinking of it as a 'murder story.' It seems, I don't know, more personal than that. It's about Becky. Someone I know . . . knew. Worked with. A friend, really."

Jerry said, "I didn't mean to sound flip or anything."

"You didn't. I'm just having trouble distancing myself . . . like a reporter is supposed to do, I guess." She stirred her spoon in the soup, her gaze on the bowl. "He wants me to do a full profile of Becky for next week's edition."

Jerry was quiet a moment. There was no sound in the kitchen except for the slight hum of the refrigerator. "You'll do a fine job," he said. "On a profile. A personal story."

"Thanks," she said. Then, "I suppose it'll be a little, you know, painful. But I want to do it."

He looked at her and nodded.

They had almost finished when the phone rang.

Elise spoke just as soon as Mary Ann picked up the handset there on the kitchen wall. "I hope I'm not interrupting anything," Elise said. "But I wanted to, well, put something out to you . . . and hope you'll take it."

Mary Ann cocked one eyebrow and got a half smile. "What

are you up to, Elise?"

Jerry had looked inquiringly at his mother, but as soon as she said "Elise" he went back to finishing his soup and sandwich, glancing up from moment to moment obviously to catch Mary Ann's end of the conversation. Jerry handled the lights and sound for the Tracks Community Theater productions. So it was natural for him to be interested in what director and overall producer Elise had to say.

Elise's rapid-fire monologue continued: "It's time we did a light comedy . . . especially after *Macbeth* in the spring. So I've decided on *Boeing, Boeing,* that madcap French comedy . . ."

Mary Ann started to say, *That's nice,* but before she could, Elise said, ". . . and I'd like you to play the part of Berthe, the crusty French housekeeper." She took a quick breath. "I hope Jerry will help build the sets as well as handle the lights and sound."

Mary Ann huffed a short laugh. "Crusty French housekeeper? So, I go from being a witch in *Macbeth* to a bitch in *Boeing, Boeing.*" Another short laugh. "Sort of type-casting me, aren't you?"

"You'd be great at it, Mary Ann. It's a fun role."

"Yes, I'm familiar with the play. Young man trying to juggle the coming and going of three different airline flight attendants."

"They're called stewardesses in the play."

"Dated," Mary Ann said. She got more serious. "But I don't know, Elise. I appreciate the offer, but you know I'm in the midst of the story about Becky Thurston . . ."

"We won't start rehearsal for at least a week. By then . . ."

"Let me think about it."

"Oh, and I'd like Phillip Mastik to play the friend, Robert, who comes to Paris to see Bernard."

"Phillip?"

"Yes. He'd be a natural. He's got a flair about him that would be perfect."

"Well, as I say, Elise, I appreciate it, but I want to think about it, at least for a couple or three days. See how things go at the paper."

"You won't have to quit your day job," Elise said with a laugh before signing off.

Mary Ann put the handset back, turned and sat at the table again. What was left of her soup was cold. Her sandwich was not quite finished. She took a small bite. "You figured what that was about," she said to Jerry.

"I'm not that familiar with the play. Maybe there was a movie? TV show? Guy's trying to keep all these women's flight schedules straightened out so he can see all of them—one at a time."

"Yes."

"Sounds like fun. You'd be great as a crusty French house-keeper." He laughed.

"Thanks. But I don't know. Right now, with—you know—Becky's story and everything I have a hard time thinking comedy."

CHAPTER NINE

Tuesday morning Mary Ann was at the paper just before eight-thirty. Ethel arrived at the same time and inclined her head in greeting. The front door was unlocked, and Thaddeus's truck was parked in the drive that extended to a loading platform at the back of the building.

Mary Ann held the front door for Ethel, and Ethel mumbled something, probably a thank-you.

Mary Ann went straight back to Thaddeus's office. He worked at his computer, tapping away on the keypad. He glanced over his shoulder at Mary Ann and hardly paused in his writing.

"Can I help you with anything?" she asked.

"I'm fine," he said. "We're in good shape. The Becky Thurston story will take up much of the front, and a jump. Using the business profile you did Friday, and Gene's piece on the school board last night will start on page one."

"Then I'll start on the Becky Thurston profile," she said.

"Good." He didn't look at her, instead frowning at something he had just written. He backed it up and rewrote.

Mary Ann got a cup of coffee, being careful not to make unnecessary noise, and went into her office. Gene was not in yet. She sat at her desk, pulled the yellow legal pad in front of her on which she'd jotted down names of some of the people she wanted to talk with about Becky Thurston. Heading the list was Sue Wilson, the head librarian. She also listed boyfriend David Lynch, and then Mr. and Mrs. Thurston, hoping they'd be willing to talk with her. She didn't feel all that comfortable about calling them, and decided she'd do that Wednesday, after she'd talked with Sue and others.

But before she started writing, she clicked on the Internet and searched for "personality effects of opioids." And she read. As she did, she began to link Becky's behavior with some of the indications: "a feeling of euphoria," maybe some drowsiness, mental confusion. As for withdrawal symptoms, they could include muscle and bone pain, nausea . . . and severe anxiety, agitation.

Poor Becky, she thought. Maybe in having her back pain treated she had, indeed, become addicted.

And this, for some reason, led to her murder. But why? Why?

Mary Ann was determined to force herself to stop surmising, wondering about the investigation into Becky's death, and get back to what she was supposed to be doing today— writing the profile of this young woman who had fallen so far.

She exhaled a full breath, and with determination typed a headline: *Young Life Cut So Short.* It helped her to at least start a lead sentence, so she wrote: *Becky Thurston was only 27 years old when her life was brutally ended.* She frowned at that sentence, and then wrote: *Becky Thurston's life ended brutally when she was only 27 years old.*

Getting rid of the *to be* verbs, Mary Ann wrote: *At 27, Becky Thurston's life ended brutally—at the hands of an unknown assailant.*

She would come back after she got into the story and change the lead even further. In fact, possibility existed that by next week the case might not involve an "unknown assailant." Just possible.

Mary Ann began writing the body of the profile, starting with what she knew firsthand about Becky. By shortly before ten, Mary Ann stopped writing, gathered her notepad and pen and told Ethel she was heading to the library.

Ethel nodded.

Mary Ann parked her Volvo in the circular drive before the redbrick one-story library, one of the newest buildings in town, thanks in large part to a hefty donation from Justine Willis Gregory. A polished brass plaque by the front door of the library paid tribute to Mrs. Gregory. Some of the townspeople wanted the library to carry her name, but when the Library Board approached her about the matter, she insisted that the raised black letters atop the front simply proclaim Camford Courthouse Library. She did concede that under the name, the sign could carry in smaller letters "The Justine Willis Gregory Branch," adding that one of these days, after she had departed, they could add the word "Memorial" just before "Branch."

Mary Ann went in the front door, breathing in the familiar aroma of books. She thought anew how each business carried its own scent. Sue Wilson finished stamping a book for one of the patrons and smiled at Mary Ann.

Sue was a tall, thin sixty-something woman with closely tended gray hair. She had been librarian even before the new building was built. She talked about retiring "in a year or two." Becky Thurston had been scheduled to take her place.

With a questioning tilt of her head, Sue nonverbally invited Mary Ann to speak. It was if she sensed that Mary Ann was there as a reporter.

"I wonder if you have time to talk a bit," Mary Ann said. "About Becky."

Sue hesitated a moment before saying, "For the paper?"

"Yes. I'm doing a profile on Becky for next week's paper. Talking with people who knew her."

"Come on back," Sue said, indicating the glass-enclosed office behind the counter. In the office, there was one desk, a couple of straight chairs and a table with a dozen or more books on it, papers spread around. It was obviously a workroom that served partly as an office. Sue slipped around the desk and sat in a low back secretarial-type chair. She rested her long, thin arms atop the desk. Mary Ann pulled one of the chairs around to face her.

Even behind her glasses, Sue's eyes were rimmed with red. She had obviously done quite a bit of crying, probably even earlier this morning.

"I know you miss her," Mary Ann said. "It was a terrible thing."

Sue acted as though she didn't trust her emotions enough to speak. Her voice a bit unsteady, she said, "Becky was like a daughter to me." Sue bit at her lips, then looked down at the desk and took a couple of breaths. "What is it you want to know?"

"As I said, I want to do a profile of her. Talk with the people who knew her, her friends, coworkers. In a way, it'll be sort of a tribute to her."

"I understand," Sue said. "Well, she was a dedicated worker. Very professional, and she loved the library." Sue paused to study Mary Ann's face. "You knew her, of course. You worked with her on most Saturdays, and she loved the way you did story hour with the children." Sue gave a faint smile. "She especially admired the made-up stories you told the children. She remarked often that you were so creative."

"Thank you," Mary Ann whispered.

Sue continued in glowing terms and descriptions about Becky Thurston, her dedication to the library, her personality, her rapport with patrons of the library, everyone she came in contact with. It was as if she couldn't stop praising Becky.

Mary Ann dutifully took notes, jotted down pertinent quotes; all the while, however, something nagged at her. It was almost too perfect. Mary Ann wondered about the mood swings that she had noticed. She was ready to delve more deeply into Sue's recounting of Becky Thurston's many virtues.

But she didn't have to.

At that moment, Sheryl Layman, one of the library assistants, who had been ruffling through some papers on the table behind Mary Ann, stepped close to Sue's desk, just to the left of Mary Ann's elbow, and spoke up. A wavering note of agitation distorted her words, the volume low but with a tone of urgency.

"I beg your pardon for interrupting, but I couldn't help but hear, Sue, and you haven't said anything, not a word about how Becky had been acting lately." Sheryl turned her ample frame toward Mary Ann. "Becky had been mean, just plain mean, lately. Maybe not every day, but some days." She rubbed her palms on the thighs of her snug jeans. "I don't want to speak ill of the dead, but she was so different these last few weeks. Not like her old self at all."

Sue raised one of her hands, long fingers spread, as if seeking peace. "Now, Sheryl, she did seem . . . seem worried about something lately, but I really and truly didn't think she was, as you say, mean."

"I'm sorry," Sheryl said. "But she *was* mean to *me*."

A woman and her child stood patiently at the front desk. Sheryl said, "I'll get it." She went to the front desk to check the woman out.

Sue appeared to be thinking. Then she looked up at Mary Ann and said, "We all have our off days." She pursed her lips, obviously picking up her train of thought about Becky. "One of the many things that Becky did here was to strengthen the audio section. Videos as well, although we're not doing nearly as much in the videos as we did . . . as we did before so much was on computers. But audio books are big."

Sue continued talking about the work Becky did at the library, including bringing Mary Ann on for story hour with the children.

After a while, Mary Ann sensed that she had as much from Sue as she needed. She folded her notepad and stood. Sue continued sitting a moment or two. Sue said, "I'll step outside with you."

Mary Ann puzzled over that. But she said, "Fine. Another lovely fall day." She didn't know what else to say.

The two of them stepped out onto the small portico, just as an older man came in, greeting them both with a smile and a comment about the nice weather. He added, "But we better keep an eye on that storm headed this way."

When they were alone again, Sue studied Mary Ann's face as if once again organizing her words. "What I wanted to say, Mary Ann, and I didn't want to say it in there, is that I did notice how Becky had sort of . . . sort of changed, as if she was worried about something." She rubbed her hands together as if to warm them or get the circulation going. "That Friday, well just last Friday, it was obvious that Becky wasn't feeling well. She trembled and was shaky. Like she had a fever. I told her to go on home, that she looked like she was coming down with something."

Mary Ann listened intently. She didn't want to take notes for fear it might stop Sue's flow of words; but she was sure she would remember what Sue was saying. It was something Sue wanted to tell another human being.

"Before she left Friday, Becky stepped up to me. There was no one else around and she said . . . and I'll never forget it . . . she said, 'I'm going to end it.' At the time, I thought she was talking about using her mind-over-matter approach—you know how determined she could be—that she was talking about ending her feeling bad. Overcome her sickness or whatever it was."

Mary Ann watched Sue take a deep breath. For a moment it looked like Sue might cry.

"Then, Sunday morning, when my son called from the rescue squad. When he called to say that Becky was . . . was dead. I thought immediately that she had killed herself because I remembered what she said about ending it. But of course, my son went on to say that someone had killed her." She shook her head as if to rid herself of that moment of knowing. "I couldn't believe it."

Mary Ann reached a hand out and touched Sue's arm. Tears had welled in Sue's eyes. She blinked them away, touched a knuckle of her free hand to her eyelids.

Softly, and with her hand still on Sue's arm, Mary Ann said, "What do you think she really meant when she said that?"

Sue shook her head. "I don't know. Not unless it was what I thought in the beginning. That she was determined to get to feeling better." Sue got a look of concern. "Maybe I shouldn't have said that. I mean, in the paper and all."

"I'll probably not write that," Mary Ann said. "I'm just trying to do a profile of her, tell the readers what people thought of her, get a picture of her."

"Please . . . don't write it."

Now it was Mary Ann's turn to take a deep breath. "Let me talk to Thaddeus. He just might want me to keep that under wraps . . . for the time being, anyway."

Sue nodded. "I know you'll be discreet." She tried a weak smile. "She was your friend, too."

"Yes," Mary Ann said.

"I'd better get back inside," Sue said.

Mary Ann thanked her and walked slowly to her Volvo, frowning and thinking about Becky's last words to Sue.

What did she mean? Was she going to put an end to her dependence on the meds that from every indication she was taking? Or maybe, just maybe, she was going to also put an end to the supply of drugs? It's bizarre to think so, but was she going to put an end, not only to the supply but to the supplier?

She drove slowly away from the library and toward the newspaper.

CHAPTER TEN

Back at the newspaper, Mary Ann glanced in Thaddeus's empty office. He was undoubtedly in the composing room working with production to put the paper to bed. But she wanted to talk to him, to tell him what Sue had said. It would help with her own thinking to talk about it.

Mary Ann was more than a little conflicted about what she would write. She wanted to write about the investigation, about the darker side of events, and at the same time her assignment now was to do a profile of a young woman whose life was cut so short.

She went into her office and plopped in her chair. She was thankful that Gene was not there. She didn't want to have to talk to him.

After sitting there staring at her computer screen for several minutes, Mary Ann squared her shoulders, took a very deep breath, held her chin up, and phoned David Lynch at the Elizabeth City Planning Department. She needed to get on with her profile. She was not going to let anything get in her way. She was determined.

A pleasant woman at the Planning Department said David was out to lunch but had asked that if he received calls to provide his mobile number. Mary Ann jotted it down and thanked her.

Immediately she punched in Lynch's cell number. He answered after the first ring. Mary Ann identified herself and explained that she was doing a profile on Becky for next week's paper.

"You're not writing about the . . . the investigation?" He sounded guarded. Hesitant.

"Oh, no, I'm not. This is just a profile of her, what she was like. Views from people who knew her, me included," Mary Ann said.

David paused for so long that Mary Ann wasn't sure if he was going to say anything else. But then she heard him clear his throat. Maybe he was struggling with emotions? He spoke: "Tomorrow I'll be going down to Nags Head and Manteo for a couple of appointments. If you want to talk—and I'm not going to go into the investigation at all—if you want to talk about Becky and what she was like I could meet you for coffee some place at nine or nine-thirty." He paused again. "Unless driving down to the Outer Banks is too much for you."

"Oh, no, that would be perfect. Not even forty-five minutes to get there."

"What about the Front Porch Café? The one at Nags Head, over on the east side of the Bypass."

"Yes, I know where it is. I'll see you there at nine or nine-thirty."

They signed off and Mary Ann smiled with satisfaction. *Yes, forcing myself to move forward always pays off.* Now that she had accomplished that, she was determined to call Becky's parents in Kitty Hawk and see if she could see them tomorrow as well.

Mr. Thurston, Becky's father, answered with a gruff voice, as if he were prepared to put off anyone who might dare to call.

Mary Ann tried to sound upbeat, friendly, but maintain something of a business manner. She identified herself and had just started to go into her request for an interview when Mr. Thurston interrupted.

"Two other reporters have called, and we told them we were not doing any interviews."

"Well, Mr. Thurston, I was a friend of Becky's and worked part-time with her at the library, and since I'm with the local paper where she lived and worked, I thought—"

Again, he broke in. "You knew Becky?"

"Yes, sir. We were not *close* friends, but certainly friends and she was the one who brought me onto the library for story hour with the children." There was silence on his end of the line, so Mary Ann went on: "I'm just doing a profile of her for next week's paper. I'm not writing about . . . about the investigation. I'm just trying to give a word picture of what she was like."

Mary Ann waited. Then Mr. Thurston said, "Hold on a minute. Let me talk with my wife . . . with Becky's mother."

Mary Ann studied her watch. One minute. Two minutes. Three minutes approached, and then Mr. Thurston came back on the line. "Okay," he said. "We'll talk with you, but my wife wants to be able to look you in the eye. Not over the phone."

"I would like that much better, too, Mr. Thurston."

"We're in Kitty Hawk, you know."

"Oh, yes, and I've got to be down at the Outer Banks tomorrow. Would some time tomorrow be convenient for you and Mrs. Thurston? Say, eleven o'clock?"

"Eleven? That should work. We live in Kitty Hawk Landing. Let me give you that address."

"Fine," Mary Ann said, even though she already had their address. She dutifully wrote it down again.

"Do you know where Kitty Hawk Landing is?"

"Yes, sir," she said. "I'll turn onto The Woods Road and . . . I know the area. It'll be no problem, and thank you very much. I'll see you and Mrs. Thurston at eleven." She wanted to end the conversation before he could change his mind.

After she disconnected and put the phone in its cradle, Mary Ann settled back in her chair and breathed out a satisfied sigh. She was proud of herself.

Gene lumbered into their office, nodded at Mary Ann and said, "You look pleased about something."

"It's the lovely fall weather, Gene."

"Always nice before a storm . . . and afterwards, and you

know we're probably going to get something by the weekend."

"I haven't heard the weather today."

"Hurricane Jessica is headed this way." He plopped down in his chair. Half a doughnut was on a paper napkin near his computer keyboard. He picked up the doughnut and took a bite.

"I thought it was supposed to veer to the northeast and miss us."

He chewed while he talked. "They don't know, never do. Even if it does, we'll still feel some of it. Rain and wind." He eased himself back up. "I better go back in composing, see if I can help Thaddeus."

Mary Ann was glad to be in their little office alone again. She could hardly wait to tell Thaddeus about her appointments tomorrow. Those two would be the real anchors for her profile. Well, along with Sue, and some others. When she thought about Sue, the words expressed to her when the two of them stood outside the library haunted her.

Mary Ann thought about her story—what she wanted to write, and what she would in all likelihood write instead.

While she pondered over her approach to a story about Becky Thurston, she leaned back in her chair, and felt those two little worry lines come between her eyebrows. She pressed her lips together and thought and thought.

It was quiet in there. The phone rang but Ethel answered it up front. From snatches of conversation, Mary Ann gathered from Ethel's end of the conversation that it had something to do with circulation. Mary Ann went back to pondering. She started to try writing an alternate lead to her profile. Maybe that would help her formulate in her mind the approach to her story.

Thaddeus came back from the composing room, entered his office a moment. She could hear him doing something at his desk, probably checking messages. Then he left his office, came out into the tiny hallway, and turned into Mary Ann and Gene's office. He stood beside Mary Ann's desk.

She looked up at him and smiled. He peered down at her over the tops of his glasses. He returned her smile. What a pleasant face he had. A bit craggy perhaps, with some time-earned creases on his forehead and cheeks, but overall a rather handsome face.

"How's it going?' he asked.

He sounded like he genuinely wanted to know.

With enthusiasm she told him about her appointments tomorrow at the Outer Banks with David Lynch and with Mr. and Mrs. Thurston.

"Good," Thaddeus said. But he continued to look at her.

She could tell her enthusiasm had been replaced by those two little worry lines. "Well, I don't know, Thaddeus. In a way, it seems I've got this story—this profile, not exactly a 'puff' piece—and on the other hand, what I'd really like to write about is the, you know, Becky's downfall. What happened to her. Because something did. Something really did."

Slowly, Thaddeus began to nod. "I understand. You've got two stories there. For now, though, we need to just have the profile of her. After that, we'll both probably dig deeper into what we'll call her downfall. But that comes after the investigation." He paused and stared over her head, thinking. Then he looked down at Mary Ann again. "I know that's the story you want to write. Doing this background stuff on her will probably help formulate that next story in your mind."

He reached behind him and pulled over the small chair that was against the wall and sat down, not far from Mary Ann. "Let me caution you, though, Mary Ann. Don't let on too much with anyone about doing that next story, the one that will get into the prescription drugs—and maybe more drugs—and delve perhaps more deeply into her subsequent murder."

His head cocked slightly, he studied Mary Ann. His expression was soft, almost affectionate. "Remember, Mary Ann, that killer is still out there."

She stared back at him.

"And we don't know who he is," Thaddeus said.

Then he rose. "I'd better make sure all is in shape back in composing."

Mary Ann straightened in her chair. "Need any help?"

"Nope, thanks. All wrapped up, ready to go. Just want to make doubly sure before we push the button for the presses to roll, as they say in those old movies." He chuckled and turned to leave. "Good work, Mary Ann, in getting those folks to talk with you."

Late that afternoon, as she got ready to leave, she stepped into Thaddeus's office. "I'm calling it a day, Thaddeus," she said.

He turned from his computer and nodded. Then, "Just talked to Chief Dalton. Not much new on the investigation. But he did check out about prescriptions. Becky had been getting painkillers from at least two doctors. For her back, allegedly. Opioids. Powerful stuff. One of the pharmacies had refused to fill any more of them for her."

Mary Ann stood there a moment. "I wonder what she did then?"

"Yeah," Thaddeus said. "You've got to wonder. If the back pain led her to get hooked, she'd be desperate to do something, get something."

Mary Ann nodded. "It's really, well, sort of sad, Thaddeus."

He looked at her. "Yes, it is. And it didn't start out that way."

They were both silent a moment or two. Mary Ann shifted her stance and tried for something lighter. "Tomorrow? Wednesday fishing for you?"

He smiled. "I wish," he said. "But with the threat of some weather this weekend, I plan to take the boat up river quite a ways to a protective little cove I know about. Just in case."

"How will you get back? I mean, you'll be driving your boat up there and everything . . ."

He faked a frown. "You know I hadn't thought about that. I guess I could put my bicycle on the boat. Now if I had a motorcycle . . ."

"Oh, Thaddeus. Seriously. Do you need me to come get you when I get back from the Outer Banks?"

"Appreciate your concern. I've already had Gene volunteer to come get me. Actually, what we're going to do is drive my truck up there, with Gene following. Park my truck and ride back to the marina with Gene. So all set." He continued smiling at her. "Maybe next week things will be slow enough that on Wednesday we can go fishing again."

"That would be nice," she said.

"All right, Ace Reporter, do a good job tomorrow. I know you will."

"Thanks."

"And, Mary Ann?"

"Yes?"

"I'm glad you signed on."

She actually blushed. "Thank you, Thaddeus. I'm enjoying it." She added, ". . . most of the time."

"Go on home."

"I'll check with you when I get back tomorrow."

CHAPTER ELEVEN

When she got home and went upstairs to her bedroom, the first thing Mary Ann did was to select what she would wear tomorrow. Look casual enough to be a working reporter, yet neat and professional enough to show she meant business. Tailored slacks again. Not her usual golf shirt. A modest blouse or better still an oxford-weave button-down short-sleeve shirt. Maybe wear or carry a lightweight white cotton sweater.

Then she stripped off what she had worn to work today, freshened up in the bathroom. Looking in the mirror, she shook her head at that one lock of hair on the right that always sprung out as if it had an independence from any of its sisters on the rest of her head. She patted at it, squinted her eyes like a dare, and sure enough, it sprang right back out again. "Heck with it," she muttered.

She glanced at the round wall clock in the bathroom. Close to six. Jerry would be home from Food Lion a bit after seven. She went back in her bedroom to the bureau, opened the second drawer. There were the new pajamas still in their tissue paper. *Well, some other time.* Instead she pulled out her mismatched cotton pajamas. Comfort clothes. And she had a favorite old white cotton robe she put on to wear while cooking supper.

What in the world would they have? She hadn't thought about that yet. A trip to Food Lion had to be on her schedule in the next few days. Occasionally she did ask Jerry to pick up something to bring home. But she sort of hated to do that.

She went downstairs to the kitchen. Yes, there was that

small ham steak that she had almost forgotten about. A package of frozen shoepeg corn. A salad from some of the lettuce that wasn't too wilted. Hawaiian rolls from the three or four remaining in the package. Okay, in business.

She moved around the kitchen preparing for the meal. She set the kitchen table first. *One of these days we'll have another meal in the dining room. Not tonight, though.* On the sideboard at the sink, she emptied the package of lettuce mix and started going through it, discarding those that had wilted or turned a disgusting, limp and slick brown. She made a face. The trashcan was beside the sink. She plopped the bad ones there with a vengeance. Still enough fixings for two modest-sized salads. There was a piece of a tomato in the fridge. She diced that and divided the chunks on the salad, set the bowls on the table, and retrieved two bottles of salad dressing. *I've simply got to make some salad dressing from scratch. Not tonight, though.*

She simmered the shoepeg corn in a pot on the small back burner, added a pat or two of butter, a bit of pepper, hesitated, and then sprinkled in just a pinch of sugar. She slapped down a frying pan for the ham steak. The ham would just be seared a bit because it was already fully cooked. Okay, another small dab of butter to the frying pan, give the thing a little more flavor. She didn't turn on the burner yet. She put the rolls out on a small plate.

Shortly the front door opened and Jerry arrived. Hearing the activity in the kitchen and smelling the food, he headed straight back. Mary Ann stood at the stove, giving the corn a gentle stirring. She looked over her shoulder at him.

"Welcome home," she said, adding in typical motherly fashion: "You look a little tired."

Jerry grinned. "I was feeling all right until you said I looked tired." He heaved an exaggerated sigh. "Now, maybe I'd better sit down." He sagged into one of the kitchen chairs.

"Wash your hands," she said. "We're ready to eat."

He rose and went to the kitchen sink and washed his hands, splashed a bit of water on his face. He reached for the dishtowel, but she handed him a section of paper towel in time. She served the food onto the dinner plates from the pan, giving Jerry a much larger piece of the ham steak than she took for herself. She joined him at the table.

Jerry eyed his mother. "How's Thaddeus's Number One reporter?"

"There're just two of us."

"Yeah, I guess that's right. You and Gene. Yeah, Gene. I guess you are Number One."

"That's mean." But she smiled.

More seriously, Jerry said, "Any more word on the murder investigation?"

"No. Not really." She cut a small bit of her ham. "Autopsy report." She decided not to say anything about the drugs. "Oh, I'm doing a profile on Becky and I'll be going to the Outer Banks in the morning to interview David Lynch and Becky's parents. Hopefully a few others as well."

"I've met David before," Jerry said. "Seems like a decent enough guy. A little strange, maybe."

"What do you mean, 'a little strange'?"

Jerry shrugged, concentrating on putting another dab of butter on his corn. Mary Ann watched and started to say something about already having put butter in the corn, but she didn't. "Oh, I don't know," Jerry said. "A little standoff-ish, I guess. He's into the martial arts stuff. Acts kind of proud of it."

Mary Ann nodded and kept on eating slowly, a small bite at a time. In a few moments she rose from the table and poured Jerry a refill of sweet iced tea and got more water for herself.

"I've got two classes in the morning," Jerry said. "Go back to work at three until ten."

"That'll be a long day for you," Mary Ann said. "You better get to bed early."

He grinned a bit. "And I'm already looking tired."

Mary Ann smiled. "I shouldn't have said anything. But you know how mothers are."

They finished eating and Jerry began clearing the table as

part of their agreed upon sharing of duties. "Take the trash out?" he asked.

"I think it's okay until tomorrow," she said. "Eat that last bite of corn. Hate to throw it away, and not enough to save."

"Okay," he said and scooped out the last bit with a spoon while standing.

The phone rang. They both looked at the handset. Mary Ann started toward it by the second ring. "Probably a telemarketer," she said, but then glanced at the caller ID display, a feature they had added to their phone the spring before because of a scary incident. "No telemarketer. It's Elise."

Elise sounded very upbeat. "I just naturally assume that by now you've eagerly agreed to take the role of Berthe in *Boeing Boeing*." She took a quick breath. "Seriously, I need you. No one else could pull off the crusty French housekeeper like you."

"Hold on a minute, Elise. I haven't agreed to anything yet." Mary Ann squeezed in a laugh. Then, "It's true I can be crusty. But I've got so many things going right now, not the least is my day job as a reporter. And we've got this ongoing story about poor Becky Thurston . . ."

"Yes, yes . . . that's a shame about her. Any leads? Developments?"

"No, not yet," Mary Ann said. "In addition, you know my Saturday mornings are at the library. Story hour . . . and, oh, yes, I've got a son, too." With a smile, she glanced at Jerry, who was taking in the conversation and grinning.

Elise barreled ahead: "I'll need Jerry to not only handle the sound and lights but also to help, if he will, in building the set. Lots of doors that got to open and close with flight attendants coming and going."

"I know a little about the play," Mary Ann said.

"Yes, and I'll get you the script in the next day or two, either at the newspaper or your house so you can read—your part, your role."

"Now, Elise, I haven't . . ."

"I got to go. Pizza delivery guy is at the front door. Talk

with you later." Elise hung up.

Mary Ann, still smiling and shaking her head, eased the handset back in the cradle.

"You'd be awesome in the part," Jerry said.

Mary Ann started to say something, but then got those two little worry wrinkles between her eyebrows. "She said the pizza delivery was at the door."

"Yeah?"

"It's Tuesday. The only pizza place that delivers is closed Mondays and Tuesdays."

Jerry said, "Well, you know Elise. Maybe it was the pizza delivery guy delivering himself, period."

With mock disapproval, Mary Ann said, "Now, Jerry, you know that's, well, sort of . . . sort of . . ." She couldn't help but begin a smile that faded before it really started. "Just the same, it *was* rather curious of her to say that."

CHAPTER TWELVE

Mary Ann was up early Wednesday morning, showered and dressed in the clothes she had chosen the evening before. The oxford-weave shirt she had selected had a slight crease down the front. She smoothed it out with her hand and figured once she put it on and tucked it in, with her body heat, the wrinkle would disappear.

She went downstairs before seven-thirty. Jerry, hunched over the kitchen table, ate a big bowl of cold cereal while he leafed through one of his textbooks. As usual, he was not quiet when he ate cereal because he breathed in at the same time he shoveled in a spoon of cereal. He glanced up when his mother came in, and went back to his cereal and book.

She started to say something about the noise, but decided not to.

"Gotta leave in just a minute," he said. "Eight o'clock class."

"I'll be leaving in a few minutes, also," she said. "You want something else to eat?" She couldn't help herself. "Something quieter?"

He looked up her, puzzled.

"You've got some milk on your chin," she said.

He dabbed at his chin with the palm of one hand and went back to finishing the cereal. He took his empty bowl to the sink, ran water in it.

"Just leave it," she said. "I'll get it later."

He nodded. "Thanks. I'll go to Food Lion right after class.

Work 'til ten. I'll get something to eat during break. Don't worry about supper for me."

"Have a good day," she said, at the same time trying to decide what she would eat.

He tucked his textbook under his arm and brushed a kiss on her cheek as he started to leave. "You, too."

"Jerry?" she said.

He stopped at the kitchen door and turned to her.

"I'm proud of you. I really am," she said.

He hesitated, bobbed his head and said, "Thanks." Then he grinned, "And I'm proud of you, Ace Reporter." And he was gone.

She decided on half a toasted bagel, cream cheese, and orange juice. Probably get coffee, maybe something else, at Front Porch Café when she met David Lynch.

By a few minutes after eight she was on Highway 158 headed to the Outer Banks. The sun was out, sky blue, and fairly warm already. The weather always seemed nice before—and after—a storm. There was a touch of humidity. It would be oppressive by the time the weather predicted for this weekend moved in.

She always enjoyed the short drive down to the Outer Banks. Her old Volvo was running well, thanks to the doctoring that Keith, their family friend and mechanic, did on it. He kept talking to her about buying a newer one but at the same time she knew he took a certain amount of pride in keeping her boxy station wagon running. The traffic was light. Much of the road straight as an arrow, and of course flat, like all of the surrounding countryside.

She approached the Wright Memorial Bridge, and marveled how crossing the three-mile long bridge presented ever-changing views. The waters of the Currituck Sound varied from trip to trip—sometimes flat as a lake and other times with choppy whitecaps. The sky and clouds varied as well, and the way the sunlight sparkled or highlighted the views. Today the water was a combination of metal gray with points of light dancing off the

water to the south, and what looked like one-foot waves of
brown and gray.

Mary Ann slowed to the required fifty-mile-per-hour speed
limit as she exited the bridge. She continued down the Bypass,
beyond Kitty Hawk and Southern Shores, to Kill Devil Hills—
the Wright Brothers Memorial off to her right—and then past
Eighth Street to Nags Head. She eased over to the left so she
could get into the turn lane as she approached the Front Porch
Café. Another car was behind her, crowding close as she
slowed. Well, heck with the other driver; he could go around or
just live with it. She spotted the café at the end of a strip mall
anchored by a fairly new Food Lion. Making the left, she pulled
into the parking area, found several spots available, and cut the
engine. She glanced at her watch: seven minutes after nine.
Right on time. She took her notepad and pen, her wallet, and got
out of the car, not bothering to lock it. Nothing in it anyone
would want to steal—unless they happened to be an avid col-
lector of discarded Wendy's hamburger wrappers and takeout
coffee cups.

She ordered a plain black coffee, medium size, and found a
table near the back from which she could keep an eye out for
anyone entering. A few minutes later, she decided on a cinnamon pastry she saw in the case up front. Leaving her coffee
on the table, she pointed to the pastry and the young woman behind the counter asked with a smile if she'd like it heated a bit.

"That would be wonderful." She took the pastry back to her
table after pulling out two napkins from the dispenser and a
plastic knife and fork. The cinnamon smelled heavenly and she
held the pastry close to her face for a moment, breathing it in. It
was gooey, chewy, and tasty enough to make her stomach growl
lightly in appreciation.

As she ate, she stole a quick peek at her watch. Twenty-two
minutes after nine. She couldn't help but have a nagging feeling
that David might not show. After all, he might think, despite her
assurances over the phone that this was just a profile, that Mary
Ann might be digging into the cloud of suspicion that Chief

Dalton had cast over him.

Mary Ann was finishing the last bite of the pastry when she saw David come in. He moved with an athletic grace. Glancing around, he spotted her, nodded without smiling and approached her table. She tilted her head and held out her hand but didn't rise.

He looked at her coffee. "Let me get a cup," he said. She watched him go to the front counter. His shoulders squared, posture erect. He wore nicely creased dress slacks, a trim-fitting light blue shirt and tie. He looked a lot more muscular than she recalled.

He came back with his coffee and pulled out the chair opposite her.

"I appreciate your taking the time to talk with me," Mary Ann said.

"As long as we just talk about what a wonderful person Becky was. Nothing about the investigation." He smiled with his lips, but his eyes were serious and without any nonsense.

"As I said on the phone, I'm just doing a profile of her. I will be talking with others—including her parents."

"They're nice people. Her parents."

"And I will probably add some of my own memories of her . . . of working with her."

He nodded.

Without making much of a show of it, Mary Ann slipped open her notepad and moved it in front of her. "How long had you known her, David?"

"Four years. We weren't, you know, dating that long. About two years we'd been dating." He took a careful sip of his coffee. "I was working in Elizabeth City, living in Camford Courthouse, and started going to the library for some research. Got to talking with her. After a while we started seeing each other. Regularly."

"Engaged?"

There was a hint of a blush before he answered. "No, not really. Although we'd begun talking about, you know, one of these days . . ."

"Please tell me, in your opinion, what she was like. What was it that attracted you to her in the first place?"

He tilted back in his chair, one hand on the coffee cup, moving it slightly, a soft smile beginning to play around his face, even his eyes. "She was so full of life. So full of plans. She just sparkled with things. Smart, too. Very quick mind. The greatest soft little laugh." He shrugged a bit. "Of course, she was good looking, too. I'll confess I noticed that the first time I saw her."

Mary Ann jotted down notes. Another couple came in and started to take the table next to theirs, but changed their minds at the last moment and took a table farther away.

"What did you all do? What did she like to do?"

"In the beginning, we went together to the fitness center two or three times a week . . . after we got off work. I'm with the Elizabeth City Planning Department, you know. At least for now." He tucked his head, lowered his voice. "I'm pretty sure I'll be here with the Dare County, planning. That's what my degree's in. Don't put it in the paper, yet."

Mary Ann nodded. "Sure. As I've said, this piece will just be about Becky, what she was like."

"And we did other things like couples do. A few movies, some television at her house." His eyes became downcast, any joy at the recapping dissolved, appearing to be overcome by the memory of discovering Becky that morning at her house. He took a breath and looked up at Mary Ann's face. "This is a real sad time," he said.

His eyes clouded over, not tears, but not far from it. She had a difficult time thinking he had anything to do with her death, with beating her to death. Yet, she reminded herself, he's polished enough to sound convincing.

He talked about how sharp Becky was at "Jeopardy," so quick, and other favorite TV programs; they went on picnics.

Mary Ann glanced up from her notes. "About the fitness center. I go there in the evenings fairly regularly, too, but I don't remember seeing Becky there. Of course, we could have gone at different . . ."

"She stopped going after she hurt her back."

"Her back. How did that happen?"

"Doing sit-ups on an incline board." He shook his head. "Not the thing to do."

This must have been what led to the pain pills, and likely addiction. She had to restrain herself from getting into this. *It's not the time, not the time. You'll scare him off.* But Mary Ann did permit herself to add, "Yes, at the library I remember she complained about her back once in a while."

David's eyes narrowed at her. He appeared ready to say something. She hoped he would go into the pills business without a prompt from her. Instead, his face lightened up, like maybe he forced it to. He got a quick, momentary smile, and glanced at his watch. "I'm going to have to cut this short because of my other appointments."

"I understand," Mary Ann said. "I certainly appreciate your taking the time to . . . to talk with me a bit." They both stood, but he didn't turn to leave immediately. He looked down at Mary Ann, her chin held high, but still a full head shorter. He said, "If you're being honest with me, you'll just stick to writing about Becky like she . . . like she was in the beginning." He rested one hand on the edge of the table. "She had changed some in recent months. Sort of up and down. If you worked with her you probably saw that, too."

Softly, Mary Ann said, "I did."

"That's the reason I left her house early Saturday evening." He shook his head. "I can't help but think that maybe if I'd stayed, not gotten pissed off at how she was acting, she might still be alive."

Mary Ann couldn't help herself. She said, "Or you might be dead, too."

His expression hardened, staring at Mary Ann's eyes. "I doubt that," he said. "I'm pretty handy with my fists—and feet."

Mary Ann nodded, and swallowed. She remained silent. *I*

wouldn't want to tangle with you. Thoughts welled up in her of how Becky was killed: beaten to death with fists and probably kicks as well.

He glanced at his watch again. "I've got to go." He tried to smile. "Don't want to be late with my—probably—new employers."

Mary Ann thanked him, watched him leave, and sat back at her table. Now it was her turn to check the time. Still a bit early to meet with Mr. and Mrs. Thurston. Maybe another cup of coffee? No, she'd better get something like orange juice.

But before she got up to get juice, she made a trip to the restroom. She thought about how everyone noted that Becky had changed. Hell, she'd probably become addicted to pain pills, opioids, or whatever else. No question about it, really. When she came back from the restroom, Mary Ann folded her notepad and stared across the room. *I'm not writing the story I want to write. Not yet.*

CHAPTER THIRTEEN

Mary Ann stayed at Front Porch Café, occupying that one table, until she felt uncomfortable taking the space as long as she had. Too early for lunch and getting closer to the time she could drive up to meet with Mr. and Mrs. Thurston.

She got up and made a show of leaving a dollar in the tip jar. Then she added another dollar. *I'll hit Thaddeus for expenses.* She smiled and returned the thank-you to the woman at the front.

When she opened the door to her Volvo and got in, it smelled of old vinyl and baked leather seats, maybe just a trace of Wendy's French fries. The engine started right away. Keith had done well. She drove below the speed limit in the right lane. As she approached Dare Centre, she considered a quick stop at Belk department store simply to look around, but checked the time again and decided it wasn't too early for her appointment with the Thurstons. So what if she was ten or fifteen minutes ahead of the scheduled visit.

Continuing up the Bypass, she slipped over into the inside lane after she approached Market Place shopping center and then to the left turn center lane at The Woods Road, opposite Kitty Hawk Elementary School. She loved driving down The Woods Road, admiring the undulating bike path on the right that skirted along with vegetation on one side and tall trees on the other. A mile or so down the road she made a right, wound along the curvy road and then another right. After passing Austin Cemetery, she slowed to a rolling stop to double-check

the road sign, turned left. She came to the handsome sign that
proclaimed Kitty Hawk Landing. A short distance later, and one
more turn, she began to check house numbers. As the numbers
sequenced, the Thurston house would be on the right. A canal
that led out into the sound ran behind the lots.

The Thurston house, with its two-car garage, rose high
above the ground with six or seven steps leading up to the front
porch, and front door with its intricate glass panels. She parked
in the paved driveway behind a Lexus SUV. Carrying her notepad and pen, she ascended the steps and pushed the doorbell.
She heard the musical chimes.

After several seconds, Mr. Thurston opened the door. He
was a tall man, rather trim in slacks, boat shoes, and an expen-
sive looking sport shirt. He had a full but neatly trimmed
moustache and receding mostly gray hair. He appraised Mary
Ann with a solemn expression, then smiled slightly when she
told him her name.

"Come in," he said. "Mrs. Thurston is in the breakfast
nook."

She followed him through the well-furnished living room
that appeared to be more than a showpiece because of a large
screen flat TV and a couple of comfortable leather chairs; a
folded newspaper rested on one of the seats, an open magazine
on the coffee table.

The breakfast nook adjoined the living room off to the left.
A spacious kitchen glowed with up-to-date stainless steel ap-
pliances. Mrs. Thurston sat at a large highly polished light-col-
ored wooden table. A photo album and several loose pictures
lay beside Mrs. Thurston's elbow.

Mrs. Thurston turned her face up toward Mary Ann and
forced a tired smile. Her eyes were weak and red-rimmed. She
wore a comfortable dress in a floral pattern; the dress was color-
ful enough that it contrasted with the grayish, washed out appearance of Mrs. Thurston.

Mary Ann stood near the table. "You've got a lovely
home." She glanced out the windows that graced the entire wall

facing the canal at the end of their backyard. A boat, probably a twenty or twenty-one-footer hoisted in a boatlift, was covered in a tarp and tied down securely. "Thank you for taking the time to talk with me just a little while."

"Have a seat," Mrs. Thurston said, rolling one palm toward a matching chair. Her gesture was one of weariness, yet there was a flicker of familiarity with that gesture that reminded Mary Ann of little hand movements that Becky would make.

Mary Ann heard a soft chirping. She glanced into the kitchen. A birdcage rested on a stand near the kitchen counter. Inside the cage was a gray-black little finch with touches of yellow around the sides of its head.

Her voice soft, Mrs. Thurston said, "That was Becky's bird, Curri. She brought him here to our house this summer. She said she wasn't home enough to give him the attention he needed."

Mary Ann smiled an acknowledgment. She thought about the bird pictures at Becky's house and the crystal figurine of a bird in flight.

Mr. Thurston took a seat at the other end of the table. A hand-held marine radio was in front of him, turned on, the volume very low. "Keeping track of the storm," he said. The radio made a faintly audible click as he turned it off. "I don't think we'll get more than some rain and stout winds. Sunday and into Monday. The hurricane appears to be turning east."

Mary Ann said, "Looks like you've got your boat well secured."

"Yes, it's strapped down tight."

Several seconds of silence, awkward silence. Then Mrs. Thurston pushed the photo album across to Mary Ann. "I was looking through this in case you wanted to see pictures of Becky . . ." and her voice trailed a bit. ". . . from the time she was a little thing."

Mr. Thurston spoke up, his voice much stronger than that of his wife. "Now the story you're doing is just a profile of Becky. Nothing about the . . . the investigation."

"That's correct. We just wanted to run a piece about her,

quotes from friends. That sort of thing." She paused a moment, wanting to get her words right. "That doesn't mean, sir, that the paper will not be following the investigation in subsequent reporting. But not this piece." She caught herself from saying "this *fluff* piece." *As opposed to the real story.* But she held her tongue.

"I understand," he said. His eyes were the same color as Becky's and had that slight turndown near the bridge of the nose.

Mary Ann was conscious that Mrs. Thurston watched her but hadn't said anything further. Mary Ann slid the photo album in front of her. "Thank you. I do want to see these pictures." She looked over at Mrs. Thurston. "As you know, I worked with Becky on Saturdays at the library. She is the one who recruited me for children's story hour."

Mrs. Thurston smiled faintly and nodded but didn't say anything. Mary Ann assumed that doctors had probably given her something to help her cope. She moved like someone sleepwalking. When she did speak, her voice was weak and slow.

Mary Ann began studying the photo album, turning the pages slowly. "She was a lovely baby," Mary Ann said.

"She was our flower, our blossoming flower," Mrs. Thurston said, her eyes filling with tears. "She was a blessing. Came to us in our later years. We had about given up hope of having a child." Mrs. Thurston had a wadded tissue in her right hand and she dabbed at her eyes.

From time to time, Mrs. Thurston pointed to pictures in the album, a number of them school pictures or others at the beach, birthday parties—there seemed to be a lot of birthday parties—and other social events. A few showed Becky with friends of hers.

Mrs. Thurston pointed to one of the friends. "That's Julie Dandridge. They've been friends since the fifth grade. She's still here on the Outer Banks and has called several times in the past few days. I spoke with her this morning. She said to give you her number and she'd be happy to talk with you over the phone about Becky." Mrs. Thurston handed a small piece of paper to Mary Ann. A neatly written number and the name Julie on it.

Mr. Thurston had remained quietly watching and listening. Then, when his wife paused a moment, he spoke: "Has there been any development in the investigation?"

"Well, I know it's ongoing. But as you know, I'm not really involved in the investigation."

He didn't want to let it go. "What about David Lynch? I understand the chief of police questioned him right in the beginning."

"Well, he's the one who found her . . ."

"Now, Harold," Mrs. Thurston said, "you know David was very fond of Becky and he wouldn't—I can't imagine David hurting her." With those tired, washed out eyes, Mrs. Thurston looked over at Mary Ann. "Harold has never been all that crazy about David. But I've always thought he was sweet and nice."

"He's smooth. That's for sure," Mr. Thurston said under his breath, staring down at the table.

Mary Ann thought it best not to tell them that she had interviewed David that morning.

"Oh, we're not very hospitable. Ms. Little, would you like something to drink. Harold, can you get the young lady . . ."

"I'm fine," Mary Ann said. "Thank you very much."

"Maybe some water?" Harold Thurston said.

"Well, yes. A plain glass of water would be fine," Mary Ann said. She was glad she had visited the restroom before she left Front Porch Café.

He brought her the water and a folded paper napkin to serve as a coaster. She took a sip and framed in her mind what she would ask next. "Did Becky spend a lot of time back here at the Outer Banks?"

"She did in the beginning," Mrs. Thurston said, "but then I guess she got so busy with her job at the library she didn't get back here that often." She squeezed the remnants of the tissue in her right hand. "Last few months we didn't get to see her that much." She studied her hands.

That fits the pattern. Instead, Mary Ann said, "I know she was very busy. She practically ran the library. What with Sue getting ready to retire and everything."

They talked on a while, with Mrs. Thurston making comments about the album. Mary Ann picked up one of the five-by-seven loose photos of Becky, a fairly recent picture. "Could I take this with me to probably use in the newspaper? Maybe one or two of these other ones, too? Let my editor decide which ones he wants to use. I'll take good care of them and return them to you as soon as we use them."

"I do want to get them back . . ."

"Oh, I promise you they will be returned promptly."

Mrs. Thurston looked at her husband. He nodded silently. "All right," she said.

Several minutes later, Mary Ann folded her notepad, took another sip of the water and thanked them for talking with her.

Mrs. Thurston searched Mary Ann's face. "Will you be at the funeral Saturday?"

"Yes, I plan to be."

"I don't know why she's going to be buried there at Camford Courthouse. She grew up here," Mrs. Thurston said.

"But that's where she'd made her home for almost three years," Mr. Thurston said. Then he added, "In that letter this summer she said she loved the area and wanted to be buried there if anything ever happened to her. She even mentioned the funeral home."

"I suppose so," Mrs. Thurston mumbled.

Mary Ann thought she might be able to give something to Mrs. Thurston. "I know she was close friends with Phillip Mastik, a young man who owns the funeral home where the service will be."

"Yes . . ." Mrs. Thurston said, sounding unconvinced.

Mary Ann stood, again thanking them for talking with her and promising to get the photographs back promptly and in good shape.

The husband said, "I'll see you to the door." Mrs. Thurston remained seated at the table as if she lacked the strength to rise. Her fingers caressed the photo album. Mary Ann looked at her one more time, feeling so very sorry for this grieving mother.

Mr. Thurston stepped out on the porch with Mary Ann. He towered over her. Clearing his throat, he said, "I know you're doing this profile of Becky, and we appreciate that, but I know, too, that as a reporter, you're close to the investigation into her . . . her death." His eyes bore down on her. "Please be frank with me, do you have any ideas of your own as to who did this?"

"I wish I did, Mr. Thurston." She held her chin up. "I considered Becky a friend, and for that reason—in addition to being a reporter—I'd give a great deal to know who did this terrible thing. Becky may have had some problems in the past few months, but just like everyone says, she was a sweet, innocent person."

He was quiet, looking out over his front yard, and then back at Mary Ann. "I know Becky had changed a lot in the past few months, and I can't help but think—to wonder—if maybe she was taking something that had changed her." He shook his head. "She was not the same person."

Mary Ann didn't know what in the hell she should say. It was lame, but she settled on saying, "I've gathered that others had noticed something of a change." *We're both skirting around the issue of drugs, and we know that's what was involved . . . but not in this story. Not yet.*

He kept his eyes on Mary Ann. "I hope authorities will find out who . . . who did this." Tears suddenly materialized. He controlled them by taking a deep breath. "Her death was somehow connected with how she'd changed. I know that." He put out his hand. Mary Ann took his hand. It was a firm handshake.

He turned and went back in the house.

"Thank you," Mary Ann said softly to his departing figure.

CHAPTER FOURTEEN

Mary Ann drove away from Kitty Hawk Landing feeling depressed. Sad. Angry, too, at whoever killed Becky Thurston, and angry perhaps at herself or at circumstances that prevented her from writing now about Becky's actual downfall. From writing a meaningful story. She felt absolutely wrung out. Depleted.

The image of Mrs. Thurston sitting there going over her photo album was heartbreaking. It was all the woman had left. Mary Ann couldn't help herself; tears welled in her eyes.

At Austin Cemetery she pulled to the edge of the road, stopped, and dabbed at her eyes with the back of her hand; she took a breath, controlling herself. A pickup truck approached behind her, slowed, and eased around on her left. The driver, an older man, peered over at Mary Ann and she raised a hand as a half-hearted greeting and to indicate she was okay. The truck continued slowly on its way.

She breathed in deeply through her nose and exhaled through her mouth. She did that again. Then she drove slowly forward. After she made her turns and got onto The Woods Road she began to feel a bit better. She stopped at the light at the Bypass, her blinker on to turn left. She was practically at the foot of the Wright Memorial Bridge, and when she was able to make her turn and speed up on the bridge, looking at the water of the Currituck Sound, the puffed clouds catching the sun to the west, she felt like herself again—resolutely determined to be optimistic. *Hell, all's right with the world. Well, not quite. There's that killer out there, but I have a job I love and it's a beautiful day and I have a loving son who is doing well. So quit feeling sorry about the world. Just do your job.*

After she crested the rise in the bridge and started the long trek toward the end of the bridge and Point Harbor, she decided she would have a talk—a firm talk—with Thaddeus about the story she should be writing instead of a fluff piece about Becky Thurston. That wasn't the real story. Well, it *was* what was needed now. She'd concede that.

A little more than thirty minutes later she reached Camford Courthouse. She drove past the Tracks Community Theater; she had to give Elise an answer whether she would accept the role of the French housekeeper in the upcoming play. She'd think about that later. Talk with Elise and check out the script.

She came to Wendy's on her right. It was time to eat something. Then go to the paper. Avoiding the drive-thru lane—she hated drive-thrus—she parked and went in to order: A plain cheeseburger and a small chocolate Frosty. She asked for a cup for water, also, because the Frosty would be too thick to drink with a straw; had to eat it with a spoon, certainly in the beginning. When she got her order, she sat at one of the small tables and took a spoonful of the Frosty even before she started on the hamburger. Lots of calories in the Frosty, the hamburger, too. Well, she planned to go to the fitness center this evening after work anyway. She unwrapped the hamburger and breathed in the aroma. Her stomach anticipated with a polite rumble. She was hungrier than she realized.

Eating didn't take long, and she was back in the Volvo and headed to the newspaper office. Ethel looked up at her when she entered. "Afternoon," Mary Ann said, and went straight back to her office, picking up one of the week's edition, glancing at the lead story as she walked. Taking a seat at her desk she read the piece on Becky's killing that Thaddeus had written. And written well, as she knew it would be. The story took a full third of the front page and jumped to page five. Flipping back to five, she read the rest of it. He had included several quotes from Chief Dalton, and the fact that at press time no suspects had been arrested. Mention was made of David Lynch finding the body and that he cooperated with the police, filling in what details he could. Thaddeus kept him from sounding too much like a suspect, but a discerning reader would be able to surmise as much.

She skimmed through the rest of the paper. Being familiar with most of the stories, she speed-read leads to see how Thaddeus might have edited them. It was a learning experience for her. She wanted to get better. Maybe, unspoken even to herself, to impress Thaddeus.

Folding the paper aside, she sighed and turned to her keyboard and started on her profile about Becky Thurston. She already had the lead in mind, so it began to flow pretty well. Glowing descriptions of what a sweet, intelligent, person Becky was, so giving and so full of life. Once or twice Mary Ann wrinkled her nose. She was getting the story down, but nagging at her was the rest of the story, the real story—the onset of drugs.

She stopped writing and pulled out the note Mrs. Thurston had given her with Julie Dandridge's number. Glancing at the time, she called, not expecting to get Becky's long-time friend right away. To her surprise, though, Julie Dandridge answered on the second ring.

Mary Ann identified herself and explained why she was calling. Julie seemed quite eager to talk. She added that Mrs. Thurston had notified her that Mary Ann would probably contact her. Yes, they had been friends since the fifth grade, Julie said, and they had been very close all through school and even college. Julie described Becky as having a great sense of humor, loving and giving, quite intelligent. That was much like others had described her.

But Mary Ann wanted more. "I know you and Becky were friends for many years, and you were close all that time, even after both of you finished college," she said. "But what about recently? Had you been close to her recently?"

Silence on the other end of the line for a moment. Then, "Well, no, not exactly."

"Really? When was the last time you saw her?"

Again, a pause. "It was almost exactly two months ago. She came down here. She stopped by my house—I was off that day —and she wanted me to go to the doctor's with her." Again, a pause.

"Yes?"

"I went with her. She obviously wasn't feeling well. Very nervous. She said her back was killing her." It sounded as though Julie shifted the phone. "But it really didn't go that well at the doctor's."

"What do you mean?"

"We waited a while before they called her in. She wasn't in there very long and when she came out she was upset and said, 'Let's go.' She was real snappy, cross. Angry. When we got in the car I asked her what was wrong. At first she didn't want to say anything and then she said the doctor wouldn't give her anything else for her back pain."

Mary Ann waited her out, hoping she might add a bit more.

"I didn't know she had that much of a back pain. It had been a while since I'd seen her . . ." Her voice caught, upset, verging on tears, it sounded like. ". . . and that was the last time I saw her."

"Thank you for sharing that with me, Julie."

"I just wish my last memory of her—the last time I was with her—had been happier."

"I understand," Mary Ann said.

The telephone interview went on only another minute or so. Julie said she was going to try to get to the funeral on Saturday.

After the telephone interview with Julie Dandridge, Mary Ann got up from her desk and ducked into Thaddeus's office for coffee, brought it back to her desk and sat there without drinking it. Then she started writing again.

She was two-thirds through a draft of the piece when she heard Thaddeus return. He spoke to Ethel and she said something back to him. With several message notes in his hand, he headed back toward his office. Before he went into his office, though, he stopped at Mary Ann's door.

"How did it go at the Outer Banks?" he said.

"Fine. I got the interviews and I'm working on this piece—this profile of what a sweet, lovely and giving person Becky was."

At her tone, Thaddeus cocked his head and peered over his little round glasses. He was dressed in older slacks and ratty looking boat shoes, a not-too-clean tight-fitting short-sleeve sweatshirt. He stepped into Mary Ann's office, standing close to her chair. "Yes?"

He didn't have to say more than that. She knew he had noticed the frustration in her voice. But she was determined to speak of something else first. "Did you get your boat upriver? Gene picked you up I assume?"

He stepped a little closer. "Yes, it's in that cove and tied down securely. Well protected from a strong blow, which is about all we'll get I believe." He continued looking at her. "Okay," he said. "What else?"

She tried to look somewhat noncommittal. There was only so much of an innocent expression that she could muster.

"Well, okay, Thaddeus. This story. It's not the real story and you know it." Her voice came out a little stronger than she intended. "The real story is how this promising young woman became hooked on drugs—probably opioids that everyone is up in arms about—and that, directly and indirectly, is what led to her downfall and death. Her murder. Brutal murder." She bobbed her head once, signaling that that was that.

Thaddeus continued to peer at her, keeping silent for a moment, but an amused crinkling of his eyes and a slow smile crept to his lips. "That's that, huh?" The smile blossomed. "I like your spunk, Ace. And you are absolutely right, of course. That's the real story—her downfall."

She inclined her head, waiting for the rest of what she knew was coming.

"But it's not the time to do that story yet," he said. "As I've said before, that story comes later, probably after an arrest, or if there's no arrest for a reasonable time, we'll do the story then—or, rather, you'll do the story then." He reached out and touched her shoulder briefly with the tips of his fingers. "To do that story now, before even the funeral, would not be right. The piece you're doing now will run as a sidebar to the story on the funeral." He studied her. "And I'll want you to cover the funeral."

She leaned back in her swivel chair. *He was right, of course.* For one thing, she needed more information to do justice to such a piece. Too, a story like that at this time, well, she could imagine how hard it would hit Mr. and Mrs. Thurston, who were still reeling from the death itself. Mary Ann smiled up at Thaddeus. "I know you're right. I guess I just want to get down the truth of what has happened, and I want whoever did that to Becky to be caught."

He continued to stand there a moment longer. Now that she had vented some of her frustration, she became more aware of Thaddeus himself. She realized how close he stood to her. She could sense his presence without looking at him. She breathed in and could catch a very slight aroma of perspiration, a salty, male scent, and it was not unpleasant at all. In fact, she liked it.

He picked up a sheet with a couple of leads on it that lay beside her computer.

Mary Ann looked at the blondish red hair on his arm. Despite herself, she was surprised to feel—what was it?—a tingling in her lower stomach. It had been a long time. She sensed, too, that Thaddeus was as attracted to her as she was to him. And that attraction had grown over the months, but both of them were using the utmost restraint to keep those emotions in check; not only because they were working together but knowing full well that once they gave in there would be no turning back. The anticipation, though, was certainly pleasant.

Thaddeus scanned the leads. "Fine," he said. "You've got it going." He turned to leave. "I've got to return a couple of phone messages."

She glanced at his back as he left her office. He was trim and erect. She looked him up and down. *You've got a nice tush, Thaddeus.*

CHAPTER FIFTEEN

Following up on her vow to work out tonight—countering the caloric effects of the chocolate Frosty and cheeseburger—Mary Ann headed to the West End Fitness Center after a quick stand-up meal of soup in her kitchen. She left a pan of soup for Jerry in case he hadn't eaten when he came in from work.

She recognized three of the vehicles in the West End lot as belonging to regulars. Three other cars she didn't recognize. About par for the evening. She was dressed in faded gray sweat pants, sneakers, and a loose-fitting cotton pullover shirt. She spoke to Jessica behind the desk when she signed in, and glanced at the names of others who had signed in ahead of her.

Going straight into the gym, she warmed up on one of the elliptical trainers. Easy on the knees and worked the upper body as well. Ten minutes on that, and she was breathing more heavily. Okay, time for the weight machines. First the biceps, then the triceps. A touch of perspiration stood out on her forehead and upper lip.

Mary Ann spoke to two of the women and exchanged a few words. Two men in their late fifties or sixties chatted between occupying a couple of the leg machines.

It was then, for the first time, that Mary Ann noticed police officer Boyd Crocker, working out on the free weights. With him was the relatively new female officer Lib Owens. Boyd Crocker appeared to be giving her lessons on the use of weights. Boyd was in a black tank top and tight fitting tailored sweat pants. He wore the fingerless workout gloves for weightlifting.

Boyd's muscles bulged and sheened with sweat. Lib Owens was dressed more like Mary Ann. No fashion model. But she seemed to be doing a good job of following Boyd's instructions. She was trim and attractive, despite her attire; her blonde hair was pulled back in that tight little bun Mary Ann had noticed at the press conference.

Mary Ann moved to the Roman chair with steadfast determination. It was strenuous, and usually she saved it for last, but it worked the abdomen fully, and she was paying for her chocolate Frosty. Propping herself up on the armrests, she began lifting her legs in a swinging motion. After a rep of sixteen, she rested standing on the foot bars, her forearms on the padded sidebars.

Lib Owens came over to the Roman chair. With a crooked half-smile, she said, "That one's a bitch, isn't it?"

Mary Ann nodded in agreement. "Sure is." She breathed heavily.

A grinning Boyd Crocker approached them. With the grin still plastered across his face, Crocker said, "You know the chief doesn't want you to talk to reporters."

"We were just talking about . . ." Then Lib obviously caught the tease in his voice.

"Hello, Officer Crocker," Mary Ann said. "She was just about to give me the latest on the investigation when you interrupted."

For the flicker of an instant, his face hardened, then relaxed into the grin again. "Yeah, I'll bet," he said.

He had a nice smile, but Mary Ann noticed the smile never reached his pale gray eyes. Cop eyes, she thought. But it was more than just the blank stare most police officers had mastered. His eyes seemed to drink in the light without reflecting it.

Mary Ann decided to take a stab at being a reporter: "Actually, I wish there were some real progress on the investigation. Becky Thurston was a friend of mine. I work part-time at the library. Story hour on Saturdays."

Boyd Crocker stiffened. Maybe she'd insulted him with her

reminder that there'd been no progress on the case. Then he said, "Yeah, I know." To Lib he said, "We better get back to it."

With a toss of her head, Lib did an exaggerated sigh.

Mary Ann smiled at her. She liked Lib; she didn't seem like the typical defensive, withdrawn, and somewhat suspicious police officer type.

Boyd Crocker did, though, and he was serious about Lib not talking to a reporter. Mary Ann watched them for a moment; then she started the leg swings on the Roman chair.

Thursday morning Mary Ann entered the newspaper office right at eight-thirty. Ethel was already there, with three extra bagels in front of her on her desk. "Take one," she said to Mary Ann. "And take one back to Thaddeus, if you would. Gene's not in yet."

"Well, thank you, Ethel. This is awfully nice of you." Mary Ann stood there smiling at Ethel. Beyond that crusty demeanor there was a generous heart.

"Take some cream cheese, too," Ethel said, and turned back to the papers on her desk, signaling that the "thank you's" were over.

Just the same, Mary Ann mumbled another thank you, and picked up two bagels and two tiny packets of cream cheese. She headed back to Thaddeus's office.

"Bagel time," she said.

Thaddeus looked up from his computer screen.

"Compliments of Ethel," she said.

He raised his eyebrows. "Nice," he said.

Mary Ann took the seat in front of his desk, handed him a paper napkin-wrapped bagel and a packet of cream cheese.

He opened the sliced bagel and squirted a thin spread of cream cheese on it. With a soft grin, he said quietly, "I think Ethel's taking a shine to you. You're lucky."

Mary Ann shrugged, chewing a bite of bagel. "Well, she always seems so busy."

"She is," he said. "Handling classified, circulation, routine obits." He shook his head, editing what he had just said. "That's wrong. No such thing as 'routine' obits."

Mary Ann finished chewing. "I agree, Thaddeus, certainly not to the families."

"Nor to the subject."

With a wry smile, she shook her head.

"No, really," he said. "I don't know what we'd do without Ethel. She's been here twenty years. Here with the Masterson family before I took over. She's a great inheritance."

Mary Ann nodded as she chewed. She could only finish half of her bagel. "What's up today?"

Thaddeus wiped his hands on the paper napkin. "At nine, you and I are going down to see Chief Dalton. He got the final autopsy report overnight. We'll want to talk with him about that and anything else that may have come up. I think one of the SBI agents was here yesterday. Maybe briefly. He's got their forensic report, also."

A few minutes before nine, as Mary Ann and Thaddeus started to the front, the door opened, and tall, regal Justine Willis Gregory entered, a press release of some sort in her hand. Ethel half-rose to greet her. Mrs. Gregory's presence, her bearing and her reputation, caused almost everyone—even Ethel—to treat Justine Willis Gregory as the town's royalty.

Thaddeus spoke politely to Justine. She smiled and returned his greeting. Then she looked at Mary Ann, a knowing twinkle in her eyes. "And how are you, Mary Ann?"

"Just fine, Mrs. Gregory, and I hope you are." Mary Ann knew from earlier intimations from Justine that she harbored belief, or maybe hope, that Mary Ann and Thaddeus would become a couple. *Well, not yet, anyway, Mrs. Gregory. But who knows?* Mary Ann returned the smile, and maybe just a tinge of twinkle also.

Justine handed the press release to Ethel, who sank back into her chair. "A little something from the Woman's Club," Justine said, inclining her chin toward the release she had given

Ethel. "The club is establishing a scholarship fund—a small one—for any worthy student who wants to pursue a degree in library science. A scholarship fund bearing Becky Thurston's name."

"That's very kind of you," Thaddeus said. "We'll be sure to run it prominently."

"I won't keep you," Justine said. "Looks like you and Mary Ann are in pursuit of truth and justice." She turned her head to Mary Ann. "And I look forward to seeing you back at the library when you once again regale the children with your marvelous stories."

"Well, yes, thank you," Mary Ann said, feeling a bit uncomfortable about exactly what she should say. "Of course, the library will be closed this Saturday for Becky's funeral."

Justine nodded, smiled, and put her hand back on the front door knob. "If you have any questions, Thaddeus, just give me a ring."

Her head held high, she left. Thaddeus told Ethel where they would be, and then they left together just as Justine drove away in the navy blue Lincoln Town Car.

They walked together toward the police station.

Mary Ann liked walking beside Thaddeus. At one point her left elbow brushed lightly against his wrist. She quickly tucked her arm closer to her side.

He didn't appear conscious of the touch. He studied the sidewalk, probably deep in thought about what he would ask Chief Dalton.

CHAPTER SIXTEEN

Mary Ann and Thaddeus stepped up to the counter at the police station. The place always smelled the same: a bit musty and vaguely sweaty. Or was it testosterone? The sleepy looking dispatcher nodded and buzzed the chief that Mr. Sinclair was there to see him. The chief apparently instructed that he come on back to his office.

"You know the way, sir," the dispatcher said, with a tilt of his head to the offices behind him.

"Absolutely," Thaddeus said.

Mary Ann, her chin held high, followed Thaddeus. She glared at the dispatcher as they passed behind him. *What am I? Invisible?*

Chief Dalton nodded at both of them as they came into his office. He remained somewhat slouched in his chair. With a flick of one hand he indicated the two chairs in front of his desk.

Dalton straightened his frame and picked up three papers from his desk. The pages were held with a single staple at the top left. "Printed this out last night," he said. "Final autopsy report." He shook his head. "Lot of medical mumbo-jumbo, but I get the message." He didn't offer the pages to Thaddeus but continued staring at them. He flipped one of the pages. Then the next one. He laid the report down on his desk. Looked up at Thaddeus, very briefly at Mary Ann, then back to Thaddeus. "Most of this stuff we already knew. But a couple of things sort of interesting. First, her neck was almost broken. Just a little more twisting and it would've snapped. At least that's what I gather from this. If so, if it had snapped, that alone would have killed her. But the beating busted her spleen and a bunch of other internal things."

Thaddeus said, "I remember the angle of her head. I wondered at the time about that."

"Yeah, the guy wasn't taking any chances." Dalton sighed. He appeared totally worn out. Whether this was physical or emotional fatigue, Mary Ann couldn't tell, but it was pronounced at any rate.

Dalton picked up the report again but didn't appear to read any section of it. "The other thing, they hurried up a toxicology report. Opioids in her system. No surprise there. That's what we suspected, and I confirmed with a couple of pharmacists here in town and one down at Kitty Hawk. She had prescriptions for painkillers. Opioids. Even some other things in her system—fentanyl. She was doping all right. Probably a 'cocktail' of muscle relaxer, painkiller, and anti-anxiety—Flexional, oxycodone, Xanax." Dalton shook his head and sighed.

Thaddeus adjusted his glasses, which he sometimes did when he was thinking something through. Then he said, "But none of those drugs—or any other drugs—were there at her place when we searched it."

Dalton said, "Yeah, makes you wonder if maybe robbery was the motive behind this whole thing."

Mary Ann spoke up for the first time: "Robbery? For the pills?"

"Possible," Dalton said. "On the street, those pills are like gold. Easy to get a buck a milligram for an opioid. You're looking at thirty dollars for a thirty-milligram pill. One pill. A handful of those, you've made yourself a big bundle of change."

Mary Ann raised her eyebrows. "That takes some money. Real money."

"Yeah, that's what I hate about drugs. If you're hooked, you can't work or can't hold a job, and you gotta steal to get the money to buy your fix—and if you steal long enough, somebody always gets killed." He shook his head again. "One thing leads to another. Every time."

Mary Ann shifted her position in the chair, wanting to speak again but not wanting to monopolize. She caught the tiny tilt of Thaddeus's head, tacitly giving her the go-ahead. "Well, Becky kept on working. She didn't really miss any work. Oh, maybe a day here and there. So if . . . ."

Dalton's words came on top of her pause. "Becky Thurston had money. As a matter of fact, she was withdrawing four hundred dollars a week, or just about every week, from her money market account. She also had a CD she'd moved over to money market for easier access." He looked at Thaddeus. "You're not printing any of these details yet?"

"No. Background only, Tom," Thaddeus said.

Dalton appeared satisfied. He held up another thin set of papers. "The SBI's forensic report. Not much here. They didn't find anything, and we didn't think they would. Usual sets of prints—the victim's, David Lynch's, a few others that weren't on file."

"One of the SBI agents from here in the area?" Thaddeus said.

"Naw. Wasn't Agent Twiddy from Elizabeth City. He's on leave. Agent from Raleigh I've never met before. He was as puzzled as we are—other than wanting to take another look at her boyfriend, David Lynch. Always those closest to the victim."

"So Lynch is still a person of interest," Thaddeus said.

Mary Ann knew that Thaddeus deliberately withheld that she had interviewed Lynch for her profile of Becky.

"We've checked his alibi . . . that he went to a bar or bistro, I guess it is in Elizabeth City, after he left Becky Thurston's house early that evening. He was there much of the night until about closing. Of course, that still gave him time to get back over here to . . . to do her. But we can't prove it." He pursed his lips. "But, yeah, he remains a person of interest."

Mary Ann wanted to add her opinion that he didn't strike

her as a killer; he appeared too concerned about Becky. But she could be mistaken. He could just be that smooth. She kept her mouth shut.

Thaddeus was quiet. Then he said, "One thing I know you checked in the very beginning, and that is any reports from whoever was on patrol that night, whether the officer saw anything unusual around town, around Becky Thurston's house."

"Oh, yeah," Dalton said. "With a small staff, we generally have only one officer patrolling by car from time to time during the night. And some of the neighborhoods don't get checked all that much. I mean, we don't expect a lot of stuff going on." He looked at Thaddeus. "Officer Crocker, Boyd Crocker, patrolled that night. First thing he did that morning after she was found was to say he had cruised around the downtown and most of the neighborhoods starting shortly after eleven o'clock. In fact, he went by the victim's house about twelve-fifteen and didn't see any activity." Dalton shook his head. "He did recall that some of her lights were on. Most of the other houses were mostly dark."

Mary Ann thought about the fact that Becky's house sat a couple of lots from her nearest neighbor, and it was a quiet neighborhood with very few children. Mostly middle-aged working couples or older semi-retired couples.

"So what's next, chief?" Thaddeus said.

With another shake of his head and an audible sigh, Dalton said, "Damn, I wish I knew, Thaddeus. The more days that go by the less chance we have of closing this thing." He rubbed his forehead. "It's a bitch. A real bitch." He shrugged his shoulders and tipped back in his chair. "I'm gonna lean on David Lynch a little bit more—as much as any reason, I'll have to admit—because I don't know where else to go." He got a wry half-smile. "But don't spread the word or print that the Chief of Police of Camford Courthouse hasn't got not the slightest inkling of what to do next."

Thaddeus rose from his chair, and Mary Ann followed suit. "We'll get out of your hair, Tom, but we want to thank you for spending the time to fill us in—on background only." Now it was Thaddeus's turn to shake his head. "I don't envy you."

"Yeah," Dalton said. "I don't envy myself either."

As they left his office and headed back to the front counter, Officer Boyd Crocker and Lib Owens stood just inside the counter. Lib managed a tiny smile and tilt of her head to Mary Ann. Crocker kept his face completely blank, those gray cop eyes taking them both in.

Outside, the sun was out but the wind had picked up noticeably. "By the weekend, we'll be getting that weather," Thaddeus said, studying the nearly cloudless sky.

"Calm before the . . . that kind of thing?" Mary Ann said.

They walked side-by-side for half a block in silence. Then Mary Ann said, "You think it was a robbery? A burglary gone wrong just to get her pills?"

They crossed tiny Parker Street before Thaddeus answered. "Possible. But just possible," Thaddeus said.

"Well, it seems to me that whoever did it would have to know that she had pills before . . . before risking all of that to get them," Mary Ann said. "And who would know she had pills?"

"Yes," Thaddeus said. "That occurred to me, too. Who would know?"

Mary Ann was very much aware of the physical closeness to Thaddeus as they walked slowly back to the newspaper.

Thaddeus said, "That brings to mind David Lynch again. He would know."

"Or her supplier," Mary Ann said, "if she was buying extra pills with that money she was withdrawing." Then, as they got closer to the newspaper, she said, "It would have to be someone she knew or was expecting and someone she obviously let into her house—no forced entry, as the cops say."

They approached the front steps of the newspaper. Thaddeus stopped with one foot on the first step. "But we're reporters. Not investigators. Our job is to report facts as we uncover them."

Mary Ann stood close. "I agree with that, Thaddeus. I do. But just the same I can't help but wanting to . . . to investigate Becky's murder. I can't help it." That tilt of the chin up at Thaddeus. "And I'm going to keep on . . . well, keep on keeping on looking into it."

Thaddeus smiled at her. "I know, Ace. I know. Just be careful when you do." He stared down at her, his voice soft. "This is a small town, Mary Ann. Everyone knows or thinks they know what everyone else is doing. So please, please be careful. You know he's . . ."

"Yes, I know," Mary Ann said. "That killer is still out there."

CHAPTER SEVENTEEN

Saturday morning Mary Ann dressed for the funeral. At first she selected a black dress but decided it looked just a tad too much like something she would wear in the evening. Second choice was a simple straight-line navy blue with a high neck. Not the greatest, perhaps, but it would serve. Her thin gold chain would be the only accessory. That was enough. She thought about pantyhose, which she hated, checked the remaining tan of her legs and decided she could pass. After all, the focus would certainly not be on her.

It would be on Becky Thurston's closed casket and her parents, who would be coming up from Kitty Hawk.

After she was dressed, she went downstairs to the kitchen. No more coffee for her. Maybe another piece of toast and juice. Jerry had eaten and left for work much earlier. She checked the time again.

At nine-forty she left and drove the five minutes to Phillip Mastik's Eternal Rest funeral home. A number of cars were there in the parking lot when she arrived for the ten o'clock service.

Inside the funeral home, she was greeted somberly by an older man in a black suit. He quietly pointed her way to the chapel. Up front, Phillip Mastik whispered to Mr. and Mrs. Thurston. His longish hair, complete with the peroxide blond strip, flopped across his forehead. He brushed back a lock with the palm of one hand, and patted Mrs. Thurston on the shoulder. She was dressed in dark gray and appeared to have shrunken even more than when Mary Ann had seen her earlier in the week.

Mary Ann was conscious of a heavy floral scent and the subdued sound of piped-in funereal organ music. Before moving to take a seat, she glanced discreetly around. Chief Dalton sat at the back of the chapel, giving him an overall view of the attendees. She spied Elise Duchamp about a third of the way down, an empty seat beside her. Mary Ann moved down the aisle and slid in beside Elise.

Elise smiled and moved her small purse. Mary Ann could smell a mint on Elise's breath. She realized her own mouth was dry. Nervous? Maybe. Just being at a funeral for someone she had known, worked with. Close enough to consider a friend, actually. "Do you have an extra mint? I could use one."

"Sure," Elise whispered and pulled a packet from the purse on her lap.

Mary Ann slipped the mint into her mouth. "Thanks."

Elise twisted her head slightly to get a view toward the rear. "Thaddeus Sinclair just came in. Sat next to the chief." She managed a slight, teasing smile at Mary Ann. "You want to go back and sit with Thaddeus?"

"I'm fine here," Mary Ann said, her chin up.

Other people filed in. The chapel was more than two-thirds full. Head librarian Sue Wilson sat near the front, a dark shawl draped across her rounded shoulders. The library was closed until two this afternoon in respect for Becky's funeral, and then open only until four, the usual closing time on Saturdays. Trying not to be too obvious about it, Mary Ann checked out some of the other people who attended. She was really looking for David Lynch. She saw him sitting well near the front on the far right. Empty seats on both sides of him. His head was bowed slightly.

Just before the services started, Justine Willis Gregory came in, head held high, her bearing regal as usual, and proceeded to an aisle seat just behind the Thurstons. It appeared to have been saved for her. Phillip stood there and held one palm toward the seat. Justine nodded to him and took her seat. Phillip offered her a small quick bow and then eased out of a side door at the back.

Mary Ann cast her eyes on the elegant, shiny dark casket. It sat on a red velvet-draped, rubber-wheeled stand. Mary Ann couldn't remember the name for the stand. It wasn't as ornate as a catafalque, which she associated with heads of states.

There was quiet and stillness for a moment. The minister rose from a large chair behind the casket. The service began. There was a prayer, and the minister, who Mary Ann assumed had come up from Kitty Hawk, gave a lengthy homily about "this lovely flower of a young woman who was taken from us so soon . . . but who is now in heaven with her Lord and Savior . . ." There was a hymn, maybe a second one, Mary Ann realized, and the service ended. People began to file out, following Mr. and Mrs. Thurston and the casket on its whispering rubber wheels.

Elise rose, and she and Mary Ann joined the thinning attendees up the aisle. Leaning in close to Mary Ann, Elise said softly, "You going to the cemetery?"

Mary Ann gave the barest shake of her head. "No."

Outside, the hearse idled, waiting for the Thurstons and others who would follow in their cars. Mary Ann caught a quick glimpse of David Lynch. He walked by himself. His face was flushed and what she could see of his eyes looked as though he had been crying.

Officers Boyd Crocker and Lib Owens stood at the ready to help direct the traffic. Lib moved to the center of the road to halt oncoming traffic as the entourage drove slowly away from the Eternal Rest funeral home.

Mary Ann watched them leave. She felt vaguely depleted, like it was late afternoon rather than not even close to noon. The air felt heavy. Humidity had increased. Clouds, some of them low, scuttered across the sky from the northeast. That weather was definitely coming. The wind caught at her hair—especially the one lock on the right side that would never stay under control—and she used a hand to brush it away from her face, trying to make it stay in place. No luck.

Elise, her car keys in her hand, stood beside Mary Ann. She glanced down at her feet and then at Mary Ann. "This isn't the greatest time to mention it, perhaps, but I do hope you will consider playing the housekeeper in *Boeing, Boeing.* You'd be great."

Elise's voice broke Mary Ann's reverie. "What? Oh, yes. Well, I'll admit I'm flattered, but I really hadn't been thinking about it. What with everything going on . . . and all."

"I'd like for you to at least read the script. It'd be fun. Jerry and Emma will build the sets, and Jerry will of course be in charge of the lighting and sound, once again. Oh, and Phillip Mastik has agreed to be the visiting friend of the main character. He'll be perfect. Just enough of a flair, and sort of flamboyant."

Mary Ann smiled a bit. "He is that."

"I can get you the script this weekend if you'd like."

"Well . . . well, okay. With the weather coming in, may be a good weekend to read." Mary Ann was intrigued with the idea of performing in another play—she had enjoyed the tiny part of one of the witches in *Macbeth*—and this would be more, she was certain, but it would also take more time. Just the same . . . and with Jerry active with the theater . . . It could be fun, and maybe get her thinking steered away from Becky's murder and the fact that the killer was still out there somewhere.

CHAPTER EIGHTEEN

At home, Mary Ann trudged upstairs to her bedroom. She kicked off her shoes and slipped out of the navy blue dress. She started to drape it across the back of the chair, but made a little face and then went ahead and hung it properly back in the closet. Get the shoes later. A quick trip to the bathroom and then she flopped down on the bed, wearing only her cotton panties and bra. She pulled an afghan over her, the one that Alan's mother had made for them years ago. She tried to get comfortable; then unhooked her bra and shrugged out of it, tossed it onto the foot of the bed. Rubbing the fingers of one hand across her forehead, she tried not to think about the funeral and the murder and all of that. She didn't believe she'd be able to fall asleep. But she did. And she slept for almost an hour.

When she waked, Mary Ann took a deep breath and tried to stretch her back out a bit. Then she sat hunched on the edge of the bed. "Crap," she said aloud. She flexed her shoulders. Rolled them, trying to loosen up. Felt stiff as though she'd just come from working out. Glanced at the clock. Almost two. She said, "Crap" again and stood. She couldn't find her bra at first; it had snuggled under the end of the afghan. A loose pair of slacks, an older sweatshirt, and boat shoes and she was ready to go downstairs. Had to eat a little something. She glanced at the dress shoes sitting near the foot of the bed. *I'll get you later.* But she paused. Relenting, she sighed, and bent over to pick up the shoes and put them away in the closet. Then she went downstairs.

A fresh cup of coffee was the first order of business, along with a slice of cheese and an apple she cut into bite-size pieces. She sat at the kitchen table. Tried to remember to sit up straighter, suck her stomach in. But she slouched forward again in a minute, elbows resting on the table.

She wasn't sure how long she sat there letting her mind roam over details of the funeral, the murder scene, David Lynch, and all the other people at the funeral, and she wondered whether she should at least read the script and take a close look at the role Elise wanted her to play. And she thought about Thaddeus and wondered what he might be doing this afternoon. It was none of her business, but just the same . . .

The front door opened and Jerry came in. He hollered out a hello, "I'm home."

"Back here," Mary Ann called. "You're early."

"Yep, went in early." He came back to the kitchen. He wore his nametag and Food Lion shirt. His dark hair was a little windblown. But he looked handsome and very grown up.

Pulling out a kitchen chair, he plopped down. Looking serious, he said, "How was the funeral?"

"Oh, you know. Depressing. But well attended . . . and short."

He nodded.

"Tonight?" she said. "I can fix . . ."

With a grin, he interrupted her, "Finally got a Saturday night off. Have a date with Emma." He spoke of Emma Young, another student in college with him, and a fellow-worker backstage at the Tracks Community Theater. "We're going down to Nags Head to Mulligan's. Betsy Robinson and Debo Cox are playing there. We're going to catch 'em."

Mary Ann made a tiny frown of concern. "You be careful. The weather's going to be turning, you know. Driving across the bridge and all."

"We'll be careful. The weather's not supposed to start getting bad until tomorrow. Wind's picking up a bit. Not bad."

He rose and got iced tea out of the refrigerator, poured a

glass and sat back down. "What about the play? You agreed to read for the part?"

Mary Ann did a quick glance at Jerry, those two tiny wrinkles between her eyebrows. "Oh, I don't know. With the paper and story hour and . . . and I want to keep on top of the investigation into Becky's . . ."

Jerry said, "I think it'd be good for you. And I know you'd be great in the part. Besides, probably best to start thinking about something else, not Becky Thurston's murder."

"Sort of hard not to think about it."

"Let your boss think about it."

She was quiet a moment. *He's really growing up. Now he's taking on the role of looking after his mom.* "Well, maybe the play would be fun." She put her hands down flat on the table. "Elise said she'd get me the script this weekend. I might run over there and pick it up this afternoon. Then read it over the weekend. What with the weather and all, it would be a good weekend to read."

He smiled. "Fine." He rose and rinsed his iced tea glass in the sink, put it upside down on the sideboard to dry. "I'm gonna take a shower and get dressed, ready to go."

By five o'clock Jerry was ready to go get Emma. Dusk was coming on and Mary Ann told him to please be careful. She glanced at herself in the mirror and decided that she was presentable enough to run over to Elise's for the script.

She was pleased at how well the Volvo's engine sounded. She drove west through town and out toward Elise's "little gingerbread house," as Elise described the neat bungalow she had acquired as her home.

When Mary Ann pulled into Elise's driveway, she didn't see her friend's red Mustang—she assumed it was nestled in the attached garage—but there was a shiny new pickup truck parked in front. Mary Ann slid her car to the left of the pickup and hesitated to get out. Elise obviously had company. The yellow porch light was on. Mary Ann cut her engine but still debated with herself as to whether to get out.

At that moment, however, the front door opened and Elise and a young man stepped out onto the small porch. Elise waved at Mary Ann. "Come on in," she called.

The young man appeared to be leaving.

He apparently spoke softly to Elise again and descended the three steps to the curved brick walkway and started to his truck. He was dressed in a loose-fitting shirt and windbreaker, baggy shorts. He had a short ponytail.

He looked familiar to Mary Ann.

Nodding to her without speaking, the young man approached his pickup. He opened the driver's side door. The dome light came on.

And Mary Ann saw the tattoo on his right calf. The same tattoo she had seen before: a skull with flowers twining up through the eye sockets.

It was disturbing to her, as if this individual appeared too frequently and there was something ominous about him, the way he looked, that tattoo, and then his eyes as he stared for a moment at Mary Ann. His eyes bored into her.

He didn't smile, but then very slowly a smile, more like a smirk, began to creep across his face. He shot her one more look and slipped into his front seat. The pickup's engine came on with a deep belch of smoke and sound.

CHAPTER NINETEEN

Mary Ann realized she gripped the steering wheel tightly with both hands. Elise waved again, smiling, and motioned for Mary Ann. The young man drove away. The engine made a low, throaty rumble.

Mary Ann stepped out of her car. She tried to smile at Elise as she strolled tentatively to the front steps.

"Come on in," Elise said. She sounded very cheerful, carefree. Elise laughed. "And get that look off your face."

Mary Ann stood close to Elise. She shot a look back at the driveway where the pickup had been. "That was the same man we saw . . ."

Elise held the door open and motioned for Mary Ann to enter. As they did, Elise said, "Yes, he's my pizza delivery boy."

They stood in the tastefully decorated living room with its muted gray leather sofa and matching leather chairs, two Shaker-style end tables and an oak coffee table. The room had more of a masculine look than feminine. Yet it was appealing and fitted Elise perfectly. Mary Ann could smell the heavy scent of burning incense from the foyer.

Cocking one eyebrow and tilting her head, Mary Ann said, "Pizza delivery . . . ?"

Smiling broadly, and with an exaggerated shrug, Elise said, "Maybe not exactly pizza." She sank on the sofa, the big carefree smile still there. "Have a seat." She flipped a hand toward one of the chairs.

Mary Ann sat on the edge of the chair, her feet planted flat on the floor in front of her. She continued to study Elise's face.

"Don't look so judgmental, Mary Ann," Elise said with a laugh.

"Sorry," Mary Ann said.

"Pot," Elise said. "Not pizza." She laughed again. "But both start with a 'p.'"

"I didn't know you . . . you smoked," Mary Ann said.

"You want some?"

Mary Ann shook her head. "No. No, thanks."

"It takes the edge off the day," Elise said. "You sure?"

"Yes. I tried it once years ago. It just made me sleepy. Or heavy, or something."

Elise's smile wouldn't go away. In fact, it got bigger as something seemed to dawn on her. She slapped her palms on her thighs. "The script, the script. You're going to read it! That's why you're here. Wonderful." She sprang from the sofa and headed to a small adjoining room that served as her office, then scurried back with the printed script in hand. "It's the perfect role for you," Elise said. She handed the script to Mary Ann and sat again on the sofa. She chuckled. "That expression you had on your face a minute ago looking at me, that's perfect for the perpetual expression that Berthe, the housekeeper, would have. Perfect."

Mary Ann held the script on her lap but didn't open it. "I'll read it this weekend." She looked down at her hands and then back to Elise. "That man, that *pizza delivery boy*, he's the one we saw twice at the Outer Banks. How did you . . . and I guess when did you . . . hook up with him?"

"Oh, I've known him—quite casually—for at least a year now. He lives down in Kill Devil Hills, I think. Another friend introduced him to me."

Mary Ann, the investigative reporter, emerged: "Does he deal in any other drugs?"

"Oh, I don't think so." Then Elise's eyes narrowed. "I know what you're wondering. Whether he might be involved in, you know, maybe heavy drugs—opioids or something—that went wrong, and somehow led to . . . to you know. Becky Thurston."

"I guess it's possible, isn't it?"

Elise's smile was a bit more subdued. "Not Jamie, I don't think. He's just a smalltime pot dealer. Picks up some extra money. He's not into heavy stuff. He's pretty mild-mannered. I can't picture him doing anything, you know, violent."

Mary Ann was silent. *Well, maybe not. But I wouldn't rule it out. That look he gave me was . . . was sort of cold, almost menacing.*

A moment later, Elise said, "And for the record, I'm not into anything heavy, either. I smoke—not every day—but I smoke pot and that's it. As I say, it takes the edge off the day. Helps me relax and feel better. Like a cocktail, and I only drink a glass or two of wine every once in a while, as you know."

"Oh, I'm not . . . not judging. I certainly didn't mean that," Mary Ann said. "I guess I was just thinking about the Becky Thurston case, and you've obviously heard that it's believed drugs were involved in some way."

"I'd heard rumors," Elise said. "From one of the police officers." She brightened again, beaming. "And speaking of police officers, I'm delighted that Lib Owens—pretty young thing— has agreed to read for the part of one of the airline stewardesses in the play—the American one. She's done dramatics in high school and some amateur plays."

"That's good," Mary Ann said. But she was still thinking about the pot dealer and fretting over what, if anything, she should tell Thaddeus about him. She didn't want to compromise Elise, yet she couldn't help but be torn with the thought that this "pizza delivery boy" could be a real suspect in Becky's murder. Ethically, morally, what should she do?

Elise's enthusiasm brought her back to the here and now, as Elise broke forth with, "I'm so glad you will read the script. With you, Lib, and Phillip Mastik, I'm getting the cast set. And I know who will make a terrific 'Bernard' and the other two flight attendants. Oh, it's going to come together . . . and it'll be such a fun show."

For the sake of her friend, Mary Ann tried her best to mirror some of Elise's zest for the play. "Well, I'll read the script, but . . ."

"Oh, you'll fall in love with the part. I know you will."

Mary Ann stood, the script in her hand and repeated, "I'm going to read it this weekend." She paused, tapping the script lightly against her thigh. "And let me see what else . . . how much I'll be involved with the paper and all . . . and I'll give you a yes or no this by Monday morning."

"Oh, I know it'll be a 'yes.'" Elise bounced up off the sofa and walked with Mary Ann to the front door. She hugged Mary Ann briefly.

Mary Ann could smell the sharp but woodsy scent of marijuana.

As she drove home, Mary Ann turned over and over in her mind whether to talk with Thaddeus about the pot dealer she had seen at Elise's. *Let's be real, you know there are plenty of people smoking pot and stealthily buying it from friends or part-time dealers like the tattooed "pizza delivery boy." That alone doesn't make him a suspect.*

By the time she had arrived close to the Pasquotank River, which looked black in the gathering night except for the increasing white caps on its surface, the wind was definitely picking up. She had to stop for a red light, and her Volvo rocked slightly from a burst of wind. Thinking of Jerry coming back tonight from Nags Head and crossing the three-mile Wright Memorial Bridge, she worried that the crosswinds coming off the Currituck Sound would make his driving tricky.

When she pulled into her driveway there on Sycamore Street, she made sure to leave plenty of room for Jerry to park his little truck behind her. As she approached her front steps, she stopped for a moment to look at the sky. Clouds, a shade lighter than the black sky above them, moved fast from the northeast. It was not raining yet, but it would be coming before morning she imagined. Despite the wind, the air felt thick and heavy with humidity.

She stood in the foyer deciding whether to go upstairs. She hung her light sweater on one of the pegs just inside the front door. After a quick trip to the half-bath off the kitchen, she brought her script, and a glass of iced tea, into the living room and settled on the sofa, adjusting one of the small pillows behind her back. *I've got to eat something soon. Oh, well, I'll do that later.*

Before opening the script, she stared off across the room, thinking. *No, I won't mention the pot delivery guy to Thaddeus. Not yet, anyway.*

CHAPTER TWENTY

Mary Ann settled comfortably and began to read. From the first lines of *Boeing Boeing* she was captivated. She liked the part that she would play as Berthe.

She reread the first lines again:

(Bernard and Gloria are breakfasting.)

GLORIA: Bernard darling, do you think I've time to eat another pancake?

BERNARD: *(looking at his watch)* I should think so—if you hurry. Berthe!

GLORIA: I adore pancakes for breakfast, don't you?

BERNARD: Not especially.

GLORIA: Back home, in America, all our dieticians agree that a big breakfast prevents neurosis all day long.

BERTHE: *(entering)* Did you call, Monsieur?

BERNARD: Another pancake, Berthe.

BERTHE: For Mademoiselle?

BERNARD: Please, Berthe.

BERTHE: And more of that "red stuff" to pour on it?

GLORIA: Yes, please. But it's not "red stuff." It's ketchup—very good for the complexion.

BERTHE: Well, I don't know what it's for, but I suppose it's all right. I don't like the look of it myself, but then I'm not here to reform the world.

BERNARD: Well, that's a relief . . .

Mary Ann smiled to herself, and even chuckled. Yes, she could play that part. It seemed perfect for her. She continued reading. Well, this was certainly not a bit part but she liked it, and could identify with Berthe. Lot of lines to memorize. But once you immersed yourself in the play, in the character, the lines seemed to come naturally. It would, indeed, be fun. The only question in her mind—and she looked up from the script and stared off across the room—was the demand on her time.

After all, though, the newspaper didn't take *all* that much time. *Let's admit it, though, you enjoy the newspaper, and spending time around Thaddeus is pleasant and vaguely exciting. Well, there's also the story hour at the library. That doesn't take much time. Just on Saturday mornings. And I enjoy that, too.*

Thinking about the play again, Mary Ann imagined Thaddeus watching the performance. He would enjoy it and she had to admit she would like showing off for him.

But before she started reading again, the specter of Becky's murder and the subsequent investigation crowded upon her mind. She felt those two little worry lines appear between her eyebrows. *Really, though, what is my role in that investigation? Nothing, nada. Except that I want it solved. Will my other activities in anyway slow down the investigation? Get real, Mary Ann. It's not your investigation. You're the reporter. The one who comes afterward and writes up what has happened.*

She heard a strong gust of wind. The window on the side of the living room, the window that she and Jerry had caulked more than once, rattled from the wind. They could never get it to snug up enough. She thought about Jerry driving home, and she worried about that. Glancing at her watch, she decided she needed to eat something. There was that leftover homemade vegetable-beef soup that Mrs. Purvis next door had delivered to them the day before just after Mary Ann had come home. Or was it two days ago? Well, it was still fresh enough, she was sure. And with a piece of toast. Okay, that would be it.

When she finished eating, she came back to the living

room, turned on the television. Time for "Jeopardy." Even though it was a rerun on Saturday night, she would watch it and save it for Jerry to see, too. Watching "Jeopardy" had become something of a ritual for them. Occasionally she was good at it—except when the category was mythology or some of the sports categories, and Jerry was a whiz at those and at ancient history and pop culture. And pop culture was another category she fell behind in. She could do all right with literature and characters from novels.

Too, she was fascinated with the characters who made it to "Jeopardy," and what their background was. She also enjoyed seeing what suit Alex Trebek would be wearing that night, and his tie, and wondering what in the world happened to all of those suits the next day.

After "Jeopardy," Mary Ann was back reading the play again. She read several of the sections more than once. Already, she realized, she was projecting herself into Berthe's character and just how she would deliver the lines. The facial expressions, Gaelic shrugs, hand movements and all.

After a while, when she heard the wind rattle the window again, she laid the script on the sofa beside her and went back to television to catch the weather news. The Norfolk stations would be giving extensive coverage to Hurricane Jessica and the coming storm.

True to form, the stations were giving full coverage to Hurricane Jessica; the track of which continued to take it off shore in a northeasterly direction. Nonetheless, there were dire warnings about high winds, rain, and flooding—first from the ocean, and then when the wind shifted from the sound side.

Also true to form, one of the stations had a wind-blown reporter standing out on the beach at Kill Devil Hills. The footage was shot late in the afternoon and showed the churning ocean, with high surfs, just behind him. He talked about ocean overwash expected at high tide, flooding portions of Highway 12, or the Beach Road. The reporter also mentioned tourists having to evacuate Ocracoke Island and parts of Hatteras. If the road flooded on Hatteras, there'd be nowhere the evacuees would be able to go. *They better do it fast*, Mary Ann thought.

As the wind grew stronger, the water in the sounds would be pushed into the rivers, and they might have flooding up as far as Camford Courthouse. Once the wind shifted as the eye of the storm moved farther north and east, the counter-clockwise wind would push the waters just the opposite way, lowering the level in the rivers but flooding land abutting the sounds.

At eleven o'clock, she alternated between reading the script and checking the weather. *I wish Jerry would come on home.* It wasn't ten minutes later that she heard Jerry pull his little truck into the driveway.

She sensed he had to take a tight grip of the storm door against the wind as he came in the house.

"Glad you're home," she said.

"That wind is really picking up. Rain's coming too."

"How was it crossing the bridge?"

"I could feel it with the truck." He grinned. "Kept both hands on the steering wheel." Glancing at his mother, he took a seat in the chair to her right. He had not taken off his wind-breaker. "Didn't think you'd still be up." He glanced at the script lying beside her. "I see you're reading it. Good, isn't it? You gonna take the part?"

"I think maybe so."

"That'd be great. Be fun."

Jerry rose and took off his jacket, hung it on one of the pegs in the hall.

Mary Ann raised her voice. "Emma okay? You got her home okay?"

"Oh, yes. We left a little early because of the weather. But we still got to hear Betsy Robinson and Debo." He came back into the living room. "They're fantastic."

"I'd better get ready for bed," Mary Ann said. "You work in the morning, don't you?"

"Yeah, got to go in early."

"You better get to bed, too."

He started for the kitchen, stopped, and said, "Oh, we ran into David Lynch at Mulligan's. He was celebrating taking a new job with Dare County, planning department. And he said Elise had called him tonight asking him to read for 'Bernard' in the play. Really the lead."

"Well, I know he acted in one of the other plays, a year or two ago." *Elise must have called David Lynch after I left late this afternoon.* "But celebrating? Right after Becky's funeral? Seems sort of . . . I don't know . . . ."

"Maybe not really celebrating," Jerry said. "He was there by himself." He stood still for a moment. "He's not seriously a suspect, is he?"

"Well, no, I don't think so." Mary Ann stood. "Chief Dalton talked to him a lot, I know . . . in the beginning."

Jerry turned to go to the kitchen. "I'm going to get some iced tea . . . Anyway, David will be good."

"Yes," Mary Ann said. Then, "Get the lights, will you?"

"Sure. Good night. See you in the morning."

I'll call Elise in the morning, tell her I'll take the part.

CHAPTER TWENTY-ONE

By early Sunday morning Hurricane Jessica's fringe brought even stronger winds and rain. Mary Ann stood at her bedroom window and watched the rain come down sideways. Branches of the crape myrtles between the sidewalk and street whipped in the wind. Small, brittle limbs and leaves littered the sidewalk and skittered across Sycamore Street. Gusts of wind made the windows shudder. It felt like the entire house trembled when gusts of wind smacked it. She could hear the wind, and the air smelled like electric charges.

She heard Jerry running the shower, getting ready to go out in the wind and rain to Food Lion for work. She hated that for him, and was determined to fix him breakfast—and make him eat it—before he went to work. She slipped out of the mismatched cotton pajamas she wore, more or less folded them loosely and stuck them in the third drawer of her dresser. The new pajamas, still with the white tissue paper on them, rested undisturbed in the far right of the drawer. She glanced at them. *Well, one of these nights before long.*

Putting on a pair of sweat pants she used at the fitness center and a thick, long-sleeve top, she went downstairs to the kitchen. She put bacon in the microwave, got out orange juice, English muffins, and eggs. Jerry preferred his eggs over light. The table was set, the skillet on low heat, smeared with a touch of olive oil, when she heard Jerry coming down the stairs.

"Come on and get your breakfast. You're not going out in this without eating."

Jerry came into the kitchen, grinning; he wore his yellow slicker, but it was not yet fastened, the hood pushed back. "Smells good," he said.

Mary Ann turned from the stove after starting the eggs. "Do you think they'll be open all day?"

"Oh, I expect so . . . unless it gets a lot worse."

"Well, it's pretty bad out there right now it seems to me."

"I think this is about as bad as it'll get." He hung his slicker on the back of the kitchen chair and sat down. "It's still moving off to the north and east."

She served his plate—two eggs, four strips of bacon, a toasted English muffin with butter—and retrieved a jar of strawberry preserves from the refrigerator. For herself, she had one piece of bacon, one egg (the one that came out looking not quite as perfect as the other two) and a half of a muffin. Orange juice and coffee for both of them, although Jerry rarely drank coffee.

Mary Ann watched her son eat. She enjoyed that. It made her feel good.

When he finished and left, after thanking her and giving her a slightly bacon-flavored quick kiss on the cheek, she continued sitting there a few minutes before getting up to clean the kitchen. Not that much to clean up. Another half a cup of coffee before she started. As she sat there, she thought again about Elise's so-called pizza delivery guy. She couldn't help but fret over whether indeed she should say something to Thaddeus about a person delivering pot and whether in any way it made him something of a suspect. Should she even bring it up? Last night she had told herself no. And today, it was probably the same. What would Thaddeus do or say? *No, once again, no. It's not something to bring up, not yet, anyway. Just the same, I'm going to keep that pizza delivery guy in mind. Try to find out more about him. He is dealing in drugs, and whoever killed Becky must have stolen her meds.*

Another heavy burst of rain smacked against the house. Outside the kitchen window, the large rose bush bobbed and ducked in the rain and wind as if trying to escape. Mary Ann shook her head. Then, just as suddenly, the rain and wind abated. She cocked her head and listened. It was still raining but it was not coming down sideways, at least for the moment. Less than a couple of minutes later, the rain pounded again.

She went into the living room and turned on the television. Yes, full storm coverage. The newscasters were excited, as if this was quite enjoyable for them. They knew they had full viewing. More shots of TV reporters in rain gear standing on the beach, leaning dramatically into the wind, with roiling waves behind them, a few drops of rain distorting the lens of the video cameras. There was more talk of ocean overwash and closures along Highway 12 at Hatteras, and up as far north as Kitty Hawk. Some soundside flooding was also expected later as the wind shifted. The hurricane itself continued to move north and east. Mary Ann was satisfied they had had the worst of it. She wondered about Thaddeus's boat. Surely it would be all right. And, despite herself, she wondered what he might be doing this morning, living there by himself at the edge of town. A nice, comfortable little house—older and a bit weather-beaten. She smiled: *Sort of like him.*

She turned the television volume down considerably, rose from the sofa, flexed her shoulders, and decided it wasn't too early to call Elise.

Although there was a phone in the living room—and one upstairs in her bedroom—for some reason Mary Ann preferred the one on the wall in the kitchen. She took the call there and sat in her usual kitchen chair, the one that faced the sink and the window over the sink.

Elise's number rang three times before she answered. When she answered, just before the fourth ring, she mumbled a hello.

"I hope I didn't call too early," Mary Ann said.

"Oh, no. I just had trouble going to sleep last night, with all the storm and wind and everything." Elise didn't sound nearly as exuberant as she did yesterday.

"You sure you're okay?"

"Oh, yes, yes." Then Elise began to sound more like herself. "Tell me you're going to take the part."

"Well, yes, I thought I would. If you're sure I'm right for it."

"Oh, my goodness yes." She chuckled, sounding like she was coming alive. "You're just crusty enough to be a wonderful Berthe."

Mary Ann managed a soft laugh of her own. "I see. In *Macbeth* you pictured me as one of the witches, and in *Boeing Boeing*, I'm 'crusty' enough for the French housekeeper. Oh, well, we take what we can get."

"We've got our first reading on Wednesday night. You can make it, can't you?"

"Well, yes. The paper will be out."

"Oh, David Lynch has agreed to take the lead as Bernard."

"Jerry told me."

Elise made a little clicking sound with her tongue, obviously thinking. "Only parts left are the two other stewardesses—the German and the Italian. As I said, Lib Owens will be the American stewardess . . . and these are stewardesses, as they were then, and not 'flight attendants.' And I've got five students from the college who have agreed to read for the other two." She took a deep breath and exhaled. "It's coming together. And it'll be a fun show. Time we did one, especially after heavy stuff, like *Macbeth* last spring."

Elise paused a moment before she added, "So glad you agreed to it, Mary Ann." Then another pause and Mary Ann could tell there was something else Elise wanted to say. "Ah, Mary Ann . . . I know you won't say anything about my . . . my pizza delivery boy. Will you?" Her voice was tinged with a plea.

"No, Elise. I won't." Mary Ann wrestled in her mind whether to say anything else. After a moment, she decided to express part of her thoughts: "I guess, with the investigation of Becky's murder and the fact that drugs might have been involved, I did just sort of wonder if . . . if perhaps that guy might be, you know, involved . . ."

Her voice level, direct sounding, Elise said, "I know that was something that went through your mind. But there's no way, I don't think, that Jamie could be involved in anything violent. I know he looks sort of disreputable, but he's just trying to make a little extra cash." She took another audible breath. "I can't imagine him as a suspect."

But I can, indeed, imagine him as certainly a person of interest, and maybe even as a viable suspect. Despite what went through her mind, Mary Ann was at a loss as to what to verbalize. So she more or less mumbled, "Well, I'm not planning to say anything about him." She tried to lighten the conversation. "Besides, if I said anything, I'd be pushed to say how I know anything about him. Don't want to do that."

"Yes," Elise said, "and I appreciate that. I figure what I do is my own business . . . and I'm certainly not hurting anyone."

Then she added, "And I don't think Jamie is the type to hurt anyone either."

CHAPTER TWENTY-TWO

When Elise and Mary Ann disconnected, Mary Ann sat there at the kitchen table without putting the handset back in its cradle on the wall. She stared at the phone, thinking, and then jumped, startled, when the phone rang. Without looking at the caller ID, thinking it was Elise phoning back with one more comment, Mary Ann answered the phone with, "Yes?"

"I was just checking on you to make sure all was okay at your house." It was Thaddeus.

"Oh, Thaddeus . . . Yes, thank you." She'd stammered a bit, she realized. "I thought . . . well, I thought it was Elise calling back . . . about the play. She wants me to take a role in it and I said I would and I guess I thought . . . anyway . . . I hope you are doing well." Her face felt a little flushed. She sat straighter in her chair, arching her back. *I'm acting like it's a boyfriend calling.* She was determined to sound less flustered.

"Doing fine here," he said. There was the slightest chuckle in his tone. Then it was newspaper editor talk. "I'm doing a bit of checking around for this week's lead storm story. And Gene is out taking pictures." There was definitely a chuckle then. "That's the one assignment he really gets with—taking pictures of potential storm damage. And he's good at it too."

"We're not expecting too much storm damage here, are we?"

"No, don't think so. Some flooding around the river, low-lying areas. Two or more trees have come down. One is impeding traffic on the Hertford Road. Lots of broken limbs. No widespread power outages."

Mary Ann listened and knew she should add something. "Well, we're fine here . . . what would you like for me to do?"

"Nothing much today. Tomorrow I'll write the main piece —local stuff. If you can keep a check on the Outer Banks, and write that tomorrow, that would be great. Probably captions for some of Gene's photos. Spice the captions up. I figure we'll do probably a full page of photos." He paused. "You can get much of your story off radio and TV, plus a few phone calls tomorrow."

"Okay," she said. She wanted to say more, not let him go. "Your boat? You think it's okay?"

"I'm pretty sure it is." Then, "Maybe Wednesday we can run up there and drive it back. Things should be fine I'd say by tomorrow afternoon or early Tuesday at the latest." He spoke rapidly. "You want to go with me? Be fun coming back down the river. Maybe cast out a line or two."

"Well, yes, I'd like that, Thaddeus."

"We can leave a vehicle at the marina and Gene can drive us up to the cove where the boat is."

A smattering more of conversation and then they hung up. *Going with Thaddeus to get his boat. That's almost like a date. Well, sort of. Inviting me to go with him.*

With the hint of a smile on her face, Mary Ann went into the living room, turned on the television, and continued watching the storm coverage. She made notes of key points: what sections of Highway 12 were closed, areas of flooding, reports of power outages. Simultaneously, she jotted down sources she would phone to verify news items: North Carolina power, highway department, sheriff's office, police departments, and others.

By late afternoon the rain and wind had diminished considerably. Overnight, Mary Ann expected the storm to have mostly ended. She was right. When she waked the next morning, clouds still moved briskly across the sky, but patches of blue and welcomed sunshine kept peeping through.

Going into the newspaper office Monday morning (Jerry

was still at home because classes had been delayed two hours), the streets were wet but drying and littered with leaves and tiny branches and other detritus. She was at the office shortly after eighty-thirty. Thaddeus's truck was there, as was Ethel's older sedan.

Ethel actually smiled and greeted Mary Ann. "I see you weathered the storm."

"Oh, yes, and I hope you did as well," Mary Ann said.

Ethel continued her smile for a moment, nodded, and went back to the messages on her desk.

Mary Ann walked down the hall to Thaddeus's office. He looked up at her and smiled. He wore a long-sleeve somewhat faded plaid cotton shirt. His hair was more unruly than usual. The little round glasses reflected the overhead light. There was a green glass-shaded lamp on the edge of his desk which he rarely turned on. Mary Ann thought the lamp made his cluttered desk appear somewhat homey.

"You doing okay?" he said.

Mary Ann liked his smile; it always seemed so genuine. "I'm fine. I hope you are."

He nodded. "Yeah." He inclined his head toward the Keurig. "Coffee?"

"Yes, a small cup. You?"

He shook his head.

She went to the coffeemaker. Slipped in a fresh Sumatra packet. Pushed the button for the smallest cup. "You can save this one for another small cup," she said. With her coffee in hand, she took the chair in front of his desk. "Why don't you turn on that lamp?" she said.

"Huh? Oh." He pulled the brass swivel chain. A soft glow cast over his arms, which lay across his desk.

She took a sip of her coffee, and, after moving two paperclips, set the mug on the edge of his desk.

"I've started the roundup piece," he said. "Once again, we've dodged the bullet."

"I've got notes started. I'll have my piece by early afternoon, I think."

"Gene downloaded some of his shots to my computer. He's got some great ones."

She took another sip, and tried to do it silently, although she did have a tendency to make a slurping sound occasionally when she drank hot coffee. That never sounded very ladylike, so she did her best. "Anything further from Chief Dalton?"

Thaddeus twisted his mouth and shook his head. "Nope, nothing. I checked with him last night. Pretense of asking about the storm. But I brought up the subject. He's pretty depressed about it. Knows that every day it gets colder, harder to solve. No new leads. Nothing."

Mary Ann thought of Jamie, the "pizza delivery guy." Her inclination was to bring it up; but there was no real reason, she argued with herself, and it would be a possible awkward situation with Elise. At the same time, she made a vow to herself: *I'm going to find out more about Jamie. I'm not going to just write him off as a good ol' boy trying to pick up some extra money. I'll find out. Don't know how yet, but I will.*

Thaddeus studied Mary Ann's face. "What is it?"

She sat straighter and put her coffee back on the desk. "Oh, nothing. It's just that . . . that I wish there was some progress on the investigation. Something to go on."

He continued watching her. Finally, he said, "I know. I'd like it solved too, and I know you would . . . a colleague and all."

Mary Ann reached for her coffee. "Not yet the time to do a more in-depth piece on Becky?"

He rolled one of the pencils in the fingers of his right hand, staring at the pencil, crafting what he would say. "No, it's not. And I'm not sure we need to do it. In a sense, if we told about how she apparently had become hooked on drugs—and without an arrest of someone—then we'd just be dragging her image, her name, down." He shook his head. "I just can't see that it would serve any purpose at this time."

Mary Ann nodded.

"Maybe after an arrest . . . if there ever is an arrest," Thaddeus said.

Mary Ann stood. "I'd better get started on my piece. I've got to make a few calls, too."

Thaddeus grinned at her. "You've taken that part—the French maid—in *Boeing Boeing*, haven't you?"

"Well, I've told Elise I would." She tilted her head. "But I didn't tell you I had taken the part . . . only that Elise had asked me. How did you know?"

"I'm a reporter, Ace. I know things."

"Yes, but . . ."

"Actually, Elise came in Friday with a release calling for tryouts. She told me she was going to ask you to take the part—insist on it. I figured you'd be persuaded." He leaned back in his chair. "I saw the show once a few years ago in Washington. It's a fun play, and you'll be perfect for the part."

Mary Ann wrinkled her nose. "Yes, as a crusty French housekeeper. From a witch in one play to a fussy, bossy, maid in the next." She made an exaggerated 'humpf' sound.

That grin of his remained, but softened a bit. "For what it's worth, Mary Ann, I don't think of you as 'crusty' . . . nor as a witch."

Now she grinned. "I guess that's some sort of a compliment?"

Thaddeus nodded. "It is."

She managed a shrug and, flustered, left his office. In the hallway she could see bright sunlight coming in through the glass of the front door. The storm had truly moved out.

Mary Ann felt buoyed, happy, complimented. It was a nice feeling. She stood for a moment looking at the sunshine coming in the door.

She was just about to turn and go into her office when she saw the pickup truck parked across the street from the office. She stepped closer to the front door, looking out through the glass. She was conscious that Ethel had glanced up at her and then gone back to what she was doing.

The truck was familiar. She was sure it was Jamie's. But the way the sun hit the truck's windows, she couldn't see the person clearly who sat in the driver's seat. She thought about stepping outside.

Puffs of exhaust came from the truck's muffler. Its motor idling.

Then it pulled slowly from the curb. As it moved away, the reflections on the window shifted. She was sure that was Jamie at the wheel.

She turned and went into her office.

She flipped on the light because it was not as bright in there. Her hand had trembled when she reached for the light switch. She pressed her palm against her thigh.

That good feeling that had washed over her was completely gone. Ebbed away. She stood at her desk. Why was he out there? Had he followed her? Maybe it was just coincidence that he happened to be there. No, he was watching. He had to be. But why?

She did her best to put it out of her mind. She had to. But her vow to find out more about him was stronger than ever.

Obviously, the person who had brutally killed Becky Thurston, beaten her to death and almost broken her neck, was still out there.

And just maybe it was Jamie.

CHAPTER TWENTY-THREE

By forcing herself to begin working on her storm story, Mary Ann succeeded in pushing the presence of the pickup into the back recesses of her mind. And by midmorning, and after placing at least a half dozen phone calls, Mary Ann's story had taken shape. Her story centered mostly on the Outer Banks and the situation there.

She was more than halfway through when Gene Paulson bustled into the office. He wore his rain gear but it was loosened, and a baseball cap was pushed back on his head. His face was flushed from being outdoors.

"I heard you got some good shots," Mary Ann said.

"Yeah, I think so. I was out into the night and again early this morning." He grinned and hung his rain gear on the back of his chair. The baseball cap still on his head.

She could tell he had enjoyed himself. It was about the only time she had seen him excited and obviously pleased with his work.

She went back to work. By early afternoon she downloaded her story to Thaddeus. He would check with her after he had done a final edit on it. She thought about the picture page he wanted to do using Gene's shots. So she stuck her head in his office. "Want me to do the captions on Gene's pictures?" she asked.

Thaddeus looked up from his computer screen. "Please," he said. "I'm sending you the photos I've selected. Work your magic on some cutlines."

She smiled. "Thanks. I'll try." Mary Ann knew the rules that Thaddeus abided by on cutlines, or captions. He had said, "Never tell me what the viewer can already see in the picture. A 'grip-n-grin' shot of two guys shaking hands, don't tell me so-and-so shakes hands with so-and-so. I can see that. Tell me why they're shaking hands." She took that guideline to heart.

And Thaddeus also liked her flair at writing headlines. She took pride in it and loved any praise from him.

On Tuesday afternoon, the paper was wrapped up and back in the composing room, ready for the press run that evening.

By the time she got home on Tuesdays, Mary Ann was pretty well worn out and ready to relax.

Gene had already left for the day and Ethel was closing up her station. Thaddeus had just come back into his office from the pressroom. He looked tired, also. She stepped into his office, her sweater across an arm, her notepad and other essentials in the soft denim zippered satchel she carried. "I thought I would head on home . . . unless there's anything else I can do . . ." She started to add "for you," but let it drop.

"You've done well, Ace. Those were very good cutlines . . . and that was an excellent story you did." He stood with both hands on the top of his desk. He stared into her face. Softly he said, "I like having you here, Mary Ann . . . with me." As if he thought that might sound too intimate, he added: "Working with me."

"Well, I like it too, Thaddeus . . ." She smiled, picking up on his tone, and said, "Working with you."

There was a moment when they both stood their ground, their eyes locked, with nothing else either seemed prepared to say beyond what they had already said—and left unsaid.

Mary Ann bobbed her head. "Well, good night. I'll see you in the morning." She turned to leave, stopped. "Oh, your boat. Tomorrow? You still want me to go with you?"

"Yes. Be fun. We'll leave here about ten or so."

Mary Ann was still smiling when she started her Volvo. Her heart beat a little faster. Back there, in the office, they were ten feet apart, and nothing was said, but it was an intimate moment. She couldn't help but feel that it was.

That night, Elise called to remind Mary Ann that they would have a reading of some of the parts for *Boeing Boeing* Wednesday night at the Tracks Theater. That meant it would be Thursday at the earliest before she could do much about trying to check concerning Jamie.

Wednesday morning Mary Ann was up early, showered and dressed even a bit more casually than usual. No jeans. She hated them. But an older pair of tan slacks, a long sleeve cotton shirt, and a windbreaker. It might get chilly coming down the river in the boat. Thaddeus liked to open the throttle, get the boat on a skimming plane.

At the *Camford Courier* by eight-thirty, Mary Ann opened the door and stepped inside. Even though she had been in the office only twelve hours before, the scent of the place assailed her and made her feel at home: the smell of newsprint, stacked back issues, the heady smell of ink and paper never got old. She loved it.

Ethel was on the phone with someone about a classified ad. She was writing down the information and hardly glanced up at Mary Ann, who smiled briefly and nodded and headed back to her desk, taking one of the fresh newspapers. Mary Ann glanced over the layout as she walked. She quickly scanned Thaddeus's lead story and her piece on the storm effects on the Outer Banks. Then she turned to the full page of pictures. She liked the layout Thaddeus had done. Heck, she admired her zippy cutlines, too. And she had to admit that Gene had captured the spirit and essence of the storm with his photographs.

She heard Thaddeus just ending a telephone call. She gave him another minute or so, then stepped into his office for the coffee. "The paper looks great," she said.

"Yes, I'm pleased," Thaddeus said. He wasn't looking at her. She stood there with her coffee in her hand, sensing that

Thaddeus wanted to say something else. He frowned at the top of his desk. Then he looked up at Mary Ann. "That was Chief Dalton I was talking to, trying for an update."

Mary Ann came over to his desk and took the chair in front, holding her coffee mug with both hands. She said, "Yes? Anything?"

"He claims not. Still a dead-end." Thaddeus toyed with a pencil, rolling it in his fingers of one hand, looking at the pencil as if he held great interest for him.

She cleared the edge of his desk and set her coffee there. "You said 'claims' as in alleges. Like you don't quite believe him."

Thaddeus glanced up at Mary Ann, the trace of a smile on his face. Admiration for her picking up on the word "claims"? He said, "I know Tom well enough to know that something is bothering him. Something is rolling around in his head, but he doesn't want to talk about it. Not yet, anyway."

"Do you think he's got a suspect in mind?"

Thaddeus was quiet. He went back to fooling with his pencil. "I don't know. I don't but my—what? suspicion?—tells me that something is bugging him." Then Thaddeus seemed to shift gears mentally. "At any rate, we've got to do a follow up on the case for next week's paper."

Mary Ann retrieved her coffee, took a sip, as quietly as possible. "I'd like to write it," she said.

He nodded. "Yes . . ." Obviously he thought of something else. Then he brightened. "Go for the boat in about an hour?"

"Yes, suits me fine. I'm ready any time."

Shortly after nine, Gene Paulson came into the office. He turned immediately to the page with his pictures. He beamed, and picked up three more copies, tearing out the page with his pictures and carefully folded the pages and stored them in his desk.

Thirty minutes later, Thaddeus stuck his head into their office, wearing a light windbreaker. "You guys ready to go?"

Mary Ann and Thaddeus rode in his truck to the marina and

parked. Gene was right behind them. Leaving his truck and approaching Gene's car, Thaddeus got in the front passenger seat after holding the back door open for Mary Ann. Gene's sedan smelled like French fries or old hamburgers or something. Mary Ann tried not to breathe too deeply.

Thaddeus started to give Gene directions, but Gene said he remembered the way to the cove. They took a small paved road to the north of town. The road got smaller and smaller. It was still littered from place to place with leaves and small branches. A couple of miles later they slowed. Thaddeus pointed to the left, and they turned onto a dirt and gravel road toward the river. Gene had to maneuver around a couple of potholes with standing water. He drove slowly. Mary Ann scooted to the edge of her seat so she could see to the road ahead of them. Pine trees and a few hardwoods flanked both sides of the road; then the woods thinned, and they came to a flat area with some type of sagebrush and no trees. The river, dark and still, lay ahead of them.

In a protected cove, Mary Ann spied Thaddeus's canvas-covered boat, tied snugly against the bank, with lines looped around small stumps at water's edge.

They got out of Gene's car and approached the boat. Mary Ann was glad she had worn older, sturdy shoes. The ground was still a little muddy in places. The sun was out fully, hardly any clouds, and although the river was not as wide this far upstream, it was still a mighty body of water. Beyond the trees to the south sunlight glistened on the dark-colored water.

She stood close to the lines while Gene helped Thaddeus get the canvas cover off the boat. Leaves and twigs lay on the canvas and they brushed those off as they folded the cover.

"Want me to take this back to the marina?" Gene asked.

"Please. If you don't mind," Thaddeus said and handed the bulky folded canvas to Gene. To Mary Ann, Thaddeus said, "Why don't we get aboard? Gene can untie the lines, toss them to us."

Thaddeus got on the boat first. It rocked a bit when he

stepped aboard over the top of the gunwale. His legs were long enough to make the move easily. Mary Ann tried to visually judge her steps. Thaddeus stood spread-legged and reached out to her.

Carefully and slowly she moved to the edge of the water. Thaddeus leaned forward, arms outstretched. She took as wide a step as she could, hoping to clear the gunwale. With a deep breath, she launched forward. One foot brushed the top of the gunwale and then slipped to the deck as she propelled herself toward Thaddeus. The boat dipped again, and she half-fell into his arms. He grabbed her tightly and she clung to him. He pulled her aboard, still holding her. She could smell his manliness and she loved it; she loved being in his arms, and they stepped back onto the deck. Slowly he released her.

"You okay?" he said. "You made it." He chuckled. "That first step is a doozey."

She tried to laugh also. She touched his arms. "Thanks," she said. Her face was flushed. That was the closest she had ever been to Thaddeus, there in his arms. And she liked it. *Maybe I shouldn't like it as much as I did, but I did.*

An image of Alan flashed through her mind. *I loved him, and he loved me, and I know Alan would want me to move ahead with life. So I don't feel guilty about liking being close to Thaddeus. Well, at least I'm going to try to not feel guilty.*

"You two okay?" Gene called. He stood there with the canvas held bulkily in both arms.

"Fine," Thaddeus said. "Let's see if the engine will start before you leave."

"Right," Gene said. That baseball cap was perched at an angle and it made him look a little comical, standing there with the canvas in both arms and that cap at such an angle.

Mary Ann moved out of Thaddeus's way while he went back to the engine and squeezed the rubber ball on the fuel line to pump gasoline into the engine. He pulled the manual choke out a tiny bit. To Mary Ann he said, "When the engine starts, push that choke back in all the way. Okay?"

Mary Ann peered to where he had his hand. "Will do," she said.

He went forward, turned the ignition on and hit the starter. The engine tried, but didn't catch. He paused a moment, then tried it again. The engine coughed, then died. Another pause and he engaged the starter again. The engine caught, and a cloud of exhaust puffed out. Mary Ann could smell it. "Push the choke in," Thaddeus called to her. She stretched across the aft bench and shoved the choke in, the exhaust fumes even stronger. She knew her hair must smell like the exhaust now. *Well, shampoo tonight.*

The engine ran fast; Thaddeus adjusted the throttle and the engine settled down with a nice even rumble. Very little exhaust now.

Thaddeus stood at the console listening to the engine making its healthy deep-throated rumble. "Sounds good," he said. Then, "Okay, Gene, if you'd untie those lines."

"Sure," Gene said. He looked about as if for some place to put the canvas, and then went to his car and almost dropped the canvas as he tried opening the back door to stuff the canvas in. But he succeeded and came back and started on the lines, tossing them to Mary Ann and onto the boat's deck as he untied them from the stumps.

With the lines off, the boat drifted backward almost imperceptibly. Thaddeus called to Gene. "Thanks a lot. Appreciate it. You can drop the canvas off in the back of my truck at the marina."

"No problem," Gene shouted.

"I owe you a cheeseburger."

Gene grinned and ambled around to the driver's side of his car. Mary Ann watched him. She realized that Gene was probably actually her age, but he seemed older, and moved that way, too. Heck, he was probably five or six years younger than Thaddeus, but he struck her as older, and looked it. A bit spread in the middle and rear; not trim and—well—sexy like Thaddeus.

She stood at the console beside Thaddeus. He bumped the gear into reverse and eased the boat out from the cove. Sliding the gear into neutral, he let the boat slip into the slow-moving current, then turned the steering so he swung the bow around and moved the gear into forward. He kept the engine slow as he maneuvered the boat out into the middle of the river. Then he prepared to feed the engine more gas, and he looked over at Mary Ann. "Hold on," he said, and he pushed the throttle forward. The boat began to dig into the water, picking up speed. With his thumb he adjusted the tilt of the engine and pushed the rpm up to about four thousand. The boat roared away, the bow rising and then settling into a smooth plane. They sped along.

She held tight to the chrome bar of the console. She wished now she had Gene's baseball cap.

The river was smooth. As she watched the trees and occasional fields on both sides, she realized she was smiling.

"Like it?" Thaddeus said loudly.

"Oh, yes. Love it," she shouted back.

He reached out his right hand and gave her a quick pat on the shoulder.

She liked that. *He wanted me to come with him. He wanted me here with him, alone on the river. Jerry may continue to tease me, but it really is sort of like a date.*

Several times down the river—and it took them close to thirty minutes to get back to the marina—she remembered how he had held her when she stumbled aboard the boat.

She continued to smile.

CHAPTER TWENTY-FOUR

When they got to the marina and secured the boat in its slip, Thaddeus grinned at Mary Ann and said, "Next time, maybe we will go downriver a bit. Fishing should be great with the fall coming on."

"That would be wonderful," Mary Ann said. *Next time. Already he's talking about next time.*

He dropped her off at the office. He said, "You've got rehearsal tonight. You might as well take off the rest of the day." That grin again. "You've put in a full work day on the water."

"Let me get my stuff inside, check for messages, and I'll take you up on it. It's been hard work helping you drive the boat."

They went inside, both smiling.

When she got home, she went straight upstairs, peeled off her clothes and got in the shower, washing the exhaust smell out of her hair.

Later she sat on the sofa in the living room going over the script again. As she read her parts she imagined body language and facial expressions that would accompany the lines she delivered.

Shortly after five, Jerry came home. She glanced at the clock when she heard him pull up front. He had classes that morning and then had worked a half-shift at Food Lion.

He came in just as Mary Ann got up from the sofa. "I'm

going with you tonight," he said. "Elise has some pictures of past sets that have been used in the production and she wants us to construct something similar. Emma will be there, and so will Tommy, who'll do more of the real carpentry work on the set."

"She wants us there by seven," Mary Ann said. "I'll start supper."

Jerry went upstairs to his room and Mary Ann hurried to the kitchen. She had already planned what they would have: boil part of a frozen package of pierogies; add a pasta sauce of butter and cheese; sauté two or three large sausage links. A tossed salad, and they'd be in business.

She felt a little guilty about taking time away from investigating Becky's murder, but then again, Lib Owens would be at the rehearsal. Maybe Mary Ann could learn something more about the investigation from the young officer. Kill two birds with one stone. The thought assuaged her guilt.

At six-fifty they were on their way to the Other Side of the Tracks Community Theater. During performances, the cast would freeze in place if a freight train came past the converted railway station. The play would resume flawlessly after the train passed. Audiences had become used to this and seemed to take pleasure in it. Mary Ann thought again how grateful she was for the generous financial support of Justine Willis Gregory. Without her, the community theater might not exist.

Elise's red Mustang was in the parking lot when they arrived, as were three other cars and one pickup truck. As they got out and started to the stage entrance, two other cars pulled into the lot. "Got a good turnout," Mary Ann said.

Jerry nodded at one of the small cars. "That's Emma's. I believe that pickup belongs to Tommy." Emma Young had become something of a "steady" for Jerry, Mary Ann was fond of the petite yet athletic young woman, a sort of no-nonsense type who seemed to dote on Jerry, watching his every move, and working well with him backstage.

As soon as they opened the stage door and went inside, Mary Ann breathed in the backstage smells—makeup, cold cream, the scent of lumber from past sets and those to come, the musty smell of the heavy purple curtain. It was all so familiar, yet struck her anew each time she entered.

Elise stood center stage talking with Emma and the man Mary Ann figured was Tommy. Elise was showing them photographs. Jerry hurried over to join them. Mary Ann decided to go down the steps on stage right and take a seat in the front row until she was called. Several people sat near the front, and others were joining, coming in from the front entrance. Most all of those seated were young women, probably from the College of the Albemarle or young working women. Only a few young men were with them, probably boyfriends. They wouldn't be reading, she didn't think, because there were only two males in the play and Elise had already said she'd decided on David Lynch as Bernard, and Phillip Mastik as Robert, Bernard's friend.

Mary Ann sensed someone moved into the seat next to her. She turned and smiled at Lib Owens, whom Elise said would play Gloria, the American stewardess. Lib was dressed casually, certainly not in her police uniform. "Good to see you," Mary Ann said, "and congratulations."

"Thanks," Lib said. "I'm a little nervous." She rubbed her hands together. "You're playing the French housekeeper, aren't you? That's a fun role." Lib looked around. "We've got several people trying out, it looks like . . ."

"And there are just two more roles to fill," Mary Ann said. "The German and Italian stewardesses."

Lib trembled, hunching her shoulders. "Unless Ms. Duchamp decides to replace me."

"Oh, no. You've got it, I'm sure."

"Hope so."

Mary Ann was silent a moment and then turned again to Lib. "The chief letting you keep your schedule pretty clear at night?"

"He's said he would, if at all possible."

"Are you still partnering with Officer Crocker? Boyd

Crocker?"

"No." She said it quickly, with a short shake of her head.

Her response was so definite and final sounding that Mary Ann turned back to her, studying her face. But Mary Ann decided not to pursue it further.

Then, perhaps to give a bit more of an explanation, Lib said, "He likes nightshifts . . . and I don't." She said it softly, eyes toward the stage, not meeting Mary Ann's gaze.

Then on the far side of the front row, Mary Ann saw David Lynch and Phillip Mastik chatting away. Phillip laughed at something David said. Phillip raised a hand and waved to Mary Ann.

Elise stepped forward, near the footlights, center stage. Jerry, Emma, and Tommy disappeared backstage, taking the photos with them. As Elise stood there looking out at those gathered, the chattering stopped. Elise waited a few more seconds, her presence demanding attention. She wore black tights and a flowing, snug fitting dark gray top that came down mid-thigh. "Thank all of you for coming tonight. In just a few minutes we'll begin. But I wanted to tell you that there are only two more roles to be filled. As you may know, *Boeing Boeing* has only six cast members. Two males and four females . . . but it's a very, very busy show, lots of in and out of doors as Bernard shuffles his three airline stewardesses in and out of his Paris apartment, trying to keep their schedules straight."

Elise clasped her hands together, arms only slightly bent at the elbow, her shoulders squared. Her blondish hair was brushed back from her face. The footlights accentuated the lift of her breasts. She looks positively stunning, Mary Ann thought. She straightened her own shoulders, but the effect on her chest wasn't nearly as dramatic. It was hard to believe Elise was three years older. *Yes, she's sexy all right . . . and she knows it and revels in it.*

After a slight pause, Elise continued: "What I thought we would do tonight would be to have a few lines of the opening scene read by the three people already selected——Bernard, the playboy with the apartment, the American stewardess Gloria, and Berthe, the French maid. That way, those of you who are trying out for the other two places—the Italian stewardess and the German stewardess—will see what I'm striving for in the play." She smiled at the group of people scattered in the first two rows. "Now, if Gloria, Berthe, and Bernard will come up, please . . . and the rest of you, break a leg."

To Lib, Mary Ann said, "Here we go . . ." The two of them ascended the short steps onto stage right, and David Lynch came up the steps on stage left. Each of them had a script clutched in hand. Mary Ann and Lib nodded hello to David, who smiled broadly at them. Mary Ann wanted to talk with David at some point, see if Chief Dalton had, indeed, questioned him further.

Elise directed Mary Ann to step back a couple of yards and David and Lib stood there together. Elise said, "Gloria and Bernard are just finishing breakfast . . . but Gloria wants some more pancakes, so Bernard has to summon his French maid, Berthe." She stepped away from them, and said, "Okay, action."

The scene that followed was the opening segment that Mary Ann had first read. When Gloria asked for her second round of pancakes, and Berthe asked if she wanted more of that "red stuff," which Gloria explained was "ketchup" and good for the complexion, some chuckles came from the people down front.

Elise stepped forward and held up her hands for them to stop. "That was wonderful. Great job." There was a smattering of applause from the few in the audience. To the young women out front, Elise said, "Just from those few lines I think you can get the tone I'm looking for . . . Bernard is trying to hustle Gloria on her way because he has another stewardess arriving shortly, Gloria is naively innocent of this—and I love your Southern accent, Lib. And Berthe—you were great, Mary Ann, just crusty enough—is out of sorts with Bernard's women coming and going."

Mary Ann and Lib, getting an okay from Elise, took their

seats back on the front row. David stood back a few steps in case Elise needed him for the next readings. Mary Ann wanted to watch the readings to see whom Elise would choose for the Italian stewardess, Gabriella, and the German stewardess, Gretchen. Making the choices was not a job Mary Ann would like, mainly because of those she would have to reject.

Less than an hour later, Elise had made her choices for the young woman to play the Italian stewardess—a dark haired beauty from the college, whose name Mary Ann didn't catch but would certainly learn as they got on with the rehearsals—and the part of Gretchen, the German stewardess, a slightly stout young mother Mary Ann knew from the community.

Elise invited two others who had tried out to attend rehearsals in case one of the regulars had to drop out for some reason.

"Thank all of you for being here tonight," Elise said from center stage. "If at all possible, I would like to do a complete read-through of the script this Friday night. Any of you who can't make Friday night?" She cast her eyes around at each player in turn. No one objected. "Good. We'll do just a straight read-through and by next week we'll start blocking out where the action will be. Within a few days . . ." and she turned to Tommy, Jerry, and Emma . . . "we should have a rough of the set, and that'll certainly make the blocking easier, and more meaningful." The three of them nodded to Elise in unison.

"Thank you all again, and I'll see most of you Friday night at seven."

There was shuffling about as those in the audience prepared to leave. Muttered comments could be heard, and some commiseration from boyfriends whose sweeties were not chosen to play one of the roles. While David spoke to Elise, Phillip came over to Mary Ann. He stood tall and brushed his blond-streaked hair back with the palm of one hand. "I simply love you as the French housekeeper, Mary Ann," he said.

"Thanks, and I know you'll be excellent as Robert. Can't wait to see you in the role on Friday."

Phillip introduced himself to Lib. "Like your style, darling."

Lib seemed a bit taken aback. She fumbled out a thank-you.

When he bowed slightly and left, Lib turned to Mary Ann. "I know who he is. Owns that funeral home. But first time I've seen him . . . up close. He's sort of . . . sort of . . ."

"Flamboyant," Mary Ann said.

With a chuckle, Lib said, "That's it. Yes, he is." She picked up her jacket. "See you Friday."

Mary Ann was almost alone down front. Elise continued talking to Jerry, Tommy, and Emma. Elise showed them pictures or drawings of previous sets, and she used her hands pointing to different spots on the stage.

David Lynch, carrying his jacket loosely in one hand, came down front and approached Mary Ann. "You did a nice article on Becky," he said.

"Thank you," Mary Ann said. She smiled in an attempt to soften what she had wanted to say earlier. "David, I'm not trying to pry, but has Chief Dalton talked with you further? He indicated he was going to."

David sighed and stood close to Mary Ann. "He has, he has. We just keep going over the same things. He obviously doesn't have anything to . . . to talk to anyone else about. I mean, doesn't he know I want to see this thing solved more than he does?" He shook his head. "Don't mean to go on about it, but jeez, maybe there's some other direction he should be looking."

"I can understand it must be frustrating," Mary Ann said.

"It is. And I've got this new job and I don't need the hassle . . ." He canted his head toward the stage. "Not to mention this play. Need to concentrate."

"You're good in the role of Bernard."

"Thanks," he said, but it sounded automatic and he obviously was thinking of something else. He gave a short wave at Mary Ann. "See you Friday."

He exited the aisle on the other side, heading for the front door. Mary Ann took the steps on stage right and stood a few paces away from Elise, who appeared to have finished conferring with Jerry and the other two.

Jerry stepped back from Elise, and he and Emma and Tommy did a bit more talking together near the rear of the stage, pointing to different sections of the stage where their sets would go. Jerry looked over at his mother. "Be ready to go in a minute," he said.

Mary Ann nodded.

Then Elise came over to Mary Ann. She smiled at Mary Ann, but it was a smile tinged with fatigue, or worry.

"Are you okay?" Mary Ann said.

"Yes . . . yes. Just a little played out, I guess." She tried another weak smile. "No pun intended."

"It's going to go well."

"Oh, I know it will. I'm pleased with the cast . . ." Then she smiled more genuinely. "And that includes you." Just as quickly, though, the concern clouded her countenance again.

Mary Ann studied Elise's face. "What is it? Something's bothering you."

Elise looked around as if to make sure they were alone there in the center of the stage. Most of the lights were out; they stood in a pool of soft overhead glow. "You haven't said anything about . . . about Jamie Driscoll coming to my house, have you?"

"No, not a word. That's your business." Mary Ann was just getting ready to express her concern over the fact that she was convinced Jamie was parked in front of the newspaper office that day—maybe watching for her. But she waited a moment as Elise obviously had something else to say.

Elise rubbed the back of one hand with the fingers of the other, massaging, warming.

"Why?" Mary Ann said. "What's wrong?"

"He came by last night. Unannounced. I don't like that. Trying to sell me pills. He was high. First time I've seen him like that. And trying to sell me pills. I don't want anything like that."

"Like what?"

"Oh, pain pills. Opioids and fentanyl. That sort of stuff. He said he was branching out. Expanding his business."

Now it was Mary Ann's turn to hesitate. "Prescription medicines were taken from Becky's house, you know." She swallowed and tried to relax her throat. Then she said, "I think—in fact I'm sure—he parked Tuesday across the street from the newspaper, like he was watching or something."

Elise frowned. "Oh, my. That bothers me. Last night he didn't make much sense, but he wanted to know if 'that girl' who came to see me and the one at the Outer Banks was a reporter. He said can she keep her mouth shut? I, of course, said absolutely."

"I don't like this, Elise."

"Neither do I." She rubbed her palms down her thighs, as if she were drying them. "I don't think I want to have anything else to do with him."

"Please be careful, Elise."

"I will." She put a hand on Mary Ann's forearm. "You be careful, too. If he starts stalking you, tell Thaddeus or the police or somebody. I still don't think he had anything to do with, you know, Becky. But high like he was . . ."

Jerry was telling Emma and Tommy good night; then Jerry approached Mary Ann and Elise. "Not interrupting. Just letting you know that I'm ready whenever you are."

Mary Ann nodded to Jerry. To Elise, she said, "We'll keep in close touch." Elise tried a smile and nodded. "I'll get the lights," she said.

As Mary Ann and Jerry left by the back steps, Jerry said, "What was that all about? She having man trouble?"

"You could call it that," Mary Ann said.

CHAPTER TWENTY-FIVE

All the way home, Mary Ann was quiet, debating once again with herself whether to say anything to Thaddeus about what Elise had said about Jamie Driscoll "expanding his business," trying to sell pills. She couldn't help but think about the missing prescription medications at Becky Thurston's house. It was a stretch, but maybe in talking with Thaddeus . . . At least he would know what to say, whether to talk with Chief Dalton about it. If so, how much would that get Elise involved? And she'd promised Elise . . . but it had gone beyond that, especially since Jamie wanted to know about "that girl" who was with Elise.

"You're awfully quiet," Jerry said.

"Oh, just thinking about something Elise said."

She pulled into their driveway, cut the engine.

Jerry looked at his mother but didn't say anything.

They went in the house.

Mary Ann said, "I'm going to get ready for bed. You should too." Then, "You want something else to eat?"

"No, I'm fine. Good night."

In her bedroom, Mary Ann undressed slowly, as if she weren't conscious of doing it at all. She pulled out old pajamas, nestled there beside the tissue covered new ones. She slipped into the old pajamas—a faded pink bottom and an equally faded loose-fitting blue top—and made a trip to the bathroom. Afterward, she sat on the edge of the bed, still going over in her mind about Jamie and what he was up to—and specifically what he might have been up to a week ago when Becky Thurston was beaten to death.

She turned off the bedside lamp and got under the light covers.

The next morning at the *Camford Courier*, she went straight to her desk and set down her little satchel, hung her cardigan sweater on the back of her chair and strode into Thaddeus's office and the coffee pot. She said a mumbled "Good morning," got her coffee and took it to Thaddeus's desk, sat in the chair in front of his desk, took a sip (quietly) of the coffee, held her chin up, staring at Thaddeus.

With his head cocked a bit, Thaddeus studied her. They were both silent. Then Thaddeus, his head at even more of a quizzical cant, said, "Yes?"

She took a deep breath, holding her coffee with both hands. "I want to talk to you about something."

He got that half-smile, like something amused him. "I sort of figured. Way you came in here."

"Well, I apologize about that, but . . ."

He got more serious. "You don't need to apologize, Mary Ann. What is it?"

She took another breath and a sip of coffee, not concerned with whether she made an indelicate slurping noise. "There's a fellow from Kill Devil Hills up here trying to sell pills. You know, pain pills, opioids, and that sort of stuff."

"Did he try to approach you?"

"Oh, no, no. Not me." She set the coffee down on the edge of Thaddeus's desk. "But I got to thinking about how those prescriptions were missing from Becky's house and . . ." She trailed off. "He was just selling some marijuana. Now trying to sort of branch out."

Thaddeus pretended to study something on the surface of his desk, head lowered.

Mary Ann looked at his hair. *Time for him to cut his own hair again. Does look nice, though. Thick and kinky.*

Thaddeus looked up at her. "You don't smoke, do you?"

"No . . ." She held her chin up.

"He been delivering to Elise Duchamp?"

Her mouth dropped open in surprise. "How did you—"

"I'm a reporter, Mary Ann," he reminded her for the second time that week. "I know a lot of things."

"I don't want to get Elise involved in any way." Her voice had a pleading tinge to it.

"Not planning to," he said. "Do you know this guy's name?"

"Jamie Driscoll."

Thaddeus was silent.

In the lull, Mary Ann related to Thaddeus what Elise had told her about Jamie showing up at her house unannounced, high, and how he had asked about "that girl."

Mary Ann took a breath and exhaled. "Then Tuesday, I'm sure he was parked out front and I felt like he was watching this place. Maybe me."

Thaddeus frowned. "That is not good."

"I agree. I certainly do." She held her coffee mug again with both hands and raised her chin. "And I want to find out more about him."

Thaddeus took off his glasses and rubbed a lens against his shirt. "You say he's from Kill Devil Hills? A fellow I know is an investigator with the Dare County Drug Task Force. I'm going to contact him, see if this Jamie Driscoll is in their sights."

Mary Ann tilted her head, leaned forward a bit, a look of concern on her face. "You sure? Stir up something, maybe put him on alert or something?"

"Oh, no. It'll be a very discreet inquiry." He put his glasses on and studied her face. "Don't worry, and depending on what this investigator says, we should talk with Chief Dalton."

"Yes. I've been thinking about that," she said.

"In the meantime, please keep alert—and I know you will —and let me know immediately if you see him hanging around again."

She nodded. Then she rose. "I appreciate it, Thaddeus.

Everything."

He bobbed his head. "You're a real pro, Ace. I mean that."

She went into her office. The compliment was gratifying, but not enough to overcome completely her growing concerns about Jamie and the overall investigation.

At noon, Thaddeus came to Mary Ann's desk. "Lunch?"

"Sure." She put her notepad in her satchel, picked up her cardigan. "Probably won't need this," she said, referring to her sweater but decided to take it anyway.

As they started to leave, Gene ambled in carrying a Hardee's carryout and a large drink in a paper cup. He said, "Got a special called meeting of the school board tonight." It was said as perhaps an explanation for arriving at noon.

Thaddeus asked Ethel if they could bring her anything, though Mary Ann was sure he knew Ethel brought her lunch from home.

"I'm fine," Ethel said. "Thanks."

The sun was out but Mary Ann could tell that it was fall and beginning to cool off a bit. She was glad she brought her sweater. They walked side-by-side to Bunny's with no words about where to eat. Inside, they didn't see Bunny right away and one of the waitresses guided them to a table near the rear. Thaddeus exchanged brief greetings with some of the patrons who were already seated and eating.

Thaddeus wanted just water, he told the waitress, whose nametag said Karen. Mary Ann ordered sweet tea. "I can use the calories this week," she said.

The waitress looked at Thaddeus. "The usual?"

"Please."

"Reuben with Thousand Island on the side," Karen said. She had spiky red hair, a few freckles across her upper cheeks, and a friendly smile, especially for Thaddeus.

"I'll take the same," Mary Ann said.

Karen nodded and smiled a bit.

Thaddeus cocked an eyebrow at Mary Ann. "No chef salad?"

"This week I need the . . ."

". . . the calories," he finished for her.

She grinned at him. "Yes."

"Okay," he said, while they had a moment without the waitress. "I talked with my source at the Dare County Drug Task Force. He's familiar with James Driscoll. They've been watching him for some time. They know he's been selling marijuana but didn't know he wanted to branch out. However, he said they've been waiting to bring him in, hoping he will lead them to someone higher up the chain. They can nab him at any time."

Quietly, Mary Ann said, "What about him as a possible suspect in Becky's death?"

Thaddeus shook his head. "I didn't bring that up. Didn't want to." He chewed lightly on his lower lip. "I did ask him, though, did he think Driscoll might have a violent streak. He said there was no evidence of that . . . but he if starts taking his own product, he could be unstable. That's the word he used. 'Unstable.'"

The waitress brought their sandwiches. "You guys enjoy," she said, and smiled at Thaddeus.

Alone again, Mary Ann said, "I think we'd better tell Chief Dalton about this, don't you?"

Thaddeus picked up his sandwich and smiled at Mary Ann. "Yes, Ace, I do." He took a small bite of his sandwich, chewed, and swallowed. "You're turning out to be quite the investigator. That was good intelligence about Driscoll."

After they finished, Mary Ann tried to give Thaddeus money for her lunch. He shook his head, "I've got it."

"I'll get the tip," Mary Ann offered.

"I got it," he said.

She had her wallet out, her fingers pulling out some ones.

"Okay," he said, "if it'll make you feel better."

"It would," she said, that chin up a bit—not the full forward thrust, but enough for the occasion.

He smiled. "Ready to go?"

They walked the couple of blocks up to the white frame police station, with the two steps that led to the wooden porch. The station was more like an old house than a business office.

Officer Chaney, sitting behind the counter, lifted her eyes and tilted her head toward the rear. "You can go on back. He's expecting you."

As they stepped around the far end of the counter and started back to the chief's office, Thaddeus said softly, "I'd called before we left the paper."

Chief Dalton was finishing up a conversation with Officer Lib Owens, who rose from one of the chairs in front of the chief's desk and stood almost at attention. Dalton had a look of deep concern on his face. "Okay . . . officer."

"Thank you, sir," Lib said and headed for the door. She nodded to Mary Ann and barely smiled.

"Is this a bad time, Chief?" Thaddeus said.

"Huh? . . . No, no this is fine." Dalton motioned to the chairs in front of his desk.

Thaddeus and Mary Ann took seats in front of his desk. The one Mary Ann took was still warm from where Lib had been sitting.

As if anticipating a first question, Chief Dalton said, "Sorry to say nothing much new here on the Becky Thurston thing."

"Didn't think so," Thaddeus said. He adjusted his shoulders a bit. "But we wanted to give you a heads up about a person of possible interest." Thaddeus then told the chief about Jamie Driscoll who was dealing now with pills—opioids and other meds—as well as pot, and the fact that Mary Ann had a source who had alerted her to Driscoll. He told the chief that he had spoken with an investigator in Dare County about Driscoll.

Dalton frowned. "I hadn't heard that." He shook his head. You two are having more luck with looking into things that I am right now." He sighed. "I appreciate the intelligence."

Thaddeus said, "It was Mary Ann who came upon this information."

Dalton looked at Mary Ann for the first time. "Thank you," he said. He sighed audibly again. "And opioids are getting a big price on the street. They're harder and harder to get. Doctors are scared to write prescriptions for them now. Been so much publicity about them." He shook his head again. "But they're still killing people. OD-ing. About a hundred deaths a day in the U.S. from them, I read just the other day."

Thaddeus said, "Scarcity of opioids means . . ."

"Yeah, I know. Means more heroin and other stuff. Anything they can get." Dalton leaned back in his chair and made it squeak loudly. He didn't seem conscious of how much noise it made. Probably used to it.

Thaddeus spoke up again. "I guess it's a long shot, Chief, and certainly not trying to get into your business, but since those prescription meds of Ms. Thurston's went missing, and Driscoll starts expanding his business the next week, I was wondering if—you know, you might want to have a little sit-down with Jamie Driscoll."

Dalton leaned forward again, accompanied by the squeaking chair, "Long shot or not, I can use all the shots I can get." He rubbed a palm across his face, then massaged his forehead with the fingers of that same hand. It was as if he was bone tired. "Tell you the truth, too, I'm not through looking at Ms. Thurston's boyfriend, David Lynch. I understand he's taken a job in Dare County. Leaving our neighborhood." He appeared to be pondering a thought. "Moves away shortly after his girlfriend is done in . . . Not that that means anything necessarily in itself. Just sort of interesting."

"I know you've got a lot on your plate, Chief," Thaddeus said.

"Yeah . . . yeah I do. I mean not just this damn investigation that ain't really moving along, but there are all sorts of other things tugging at me—administrative and personnel sorts of things."

"We'll get out of your hair," Thaddeus said, starting to rise. So did Mary Ann.

"Oh, I appreciate the tip about Driscoll." Dalton rose too, pushing his chair back on its rollers. Addressing Thaddeus, he said, "You're about the only one around here I can bounce ideas off of. And I know you don't write what shouldn't be written . . . before it should be written. That sort of thing." He made a tired sounding chuckle. "I'm running on at the mouth," he said. "Good to see both of you."

They walked back toward the newspaper. As they crossed small Olive Street, Mary Ann said what she had been thinking of. "When he mentioned administrative and personnel issues, I got to wondering if that had anything to do with the conversation he was having with Officer Lib Owens when we went in."

"Hard to tell. But something was on his mind." Thaddeus shrugged. "Have no idea what they were talking about."

Mary Ann said, "Well, whatever it was, it had been going on a while . . . because her chair was still warm."

Thaddeus smiled at her, kept walking. "Maybe you'll find out at rehearsal."

CHAPTER TWENTY-SIX

That evening, in preparation for the full script run-through on Friday night, Mary Ann got welcome help from son Jerry. He read some of the other parts to her while she tried to recite hers—the ones she could do without squeaking out "line" so that Jerry would have to prompt her.

She was pleased with how much she had already memorized. She'd found that if she thought about the natural flow of the action, the lines came easier to her. Also, she was proud of how she had taken on the persona of Berthe. She realized she loved the role. "I'll be a star," she laughed to Jerry.

"I know you will," he said. "I don't have to work tomorrow afternoon, so Emma and I will meet with Tommy to begin constructing the set. We may have to do it very quietly when you *stars* get there and start going through your lines."

After he finished classes on Friday afternoon, Jerry grabbed a bite to eat and went on to the theater. Mary Ann spent the next few hours tracking down Jamie Driscoll on the internet. He had a Facebook page, but no other social media she could find. Scrolling down his feed past memes and videos about hot girls, legalized weed, and entertaining Labrador retrievers, she looked for any connection to Becky but came up empty. Frustrating. She glanced at the clock and reluctantly logged off, leaving home shortly before seven to join Jerry and the others. She had her script—that was getting a tad dog-eared—clutched tightly in her hand as she got in her car to drive to the theater.

She parked beside Elise's Mustang. She shrugged, looking

at the two cars there beside each other—Elise's sleek red job, and her boxy faded dark blue much older Volvo wagon. *Oh, well . . .*

Inside the stage entrance she breathed deeply. Ah, those familiar smells. Immediately, she felt at home and a little excited. She greeted Elise, who scurried about, and David Lynch, Phillip Mastik, and Lib Owens, who sat hunched on a fold-up chair engrossed in leafing through her script. She wore sweat pants and a loose top, sneakers. A far cry from the uniform she donned so smartly in Chief Dalton's office the day before.

Mary Ann made a point of introducing herself to the two other players, Valerie Volker, who would play the German stewardess Gretchen, and Pam-something who was selected as the Italian airline stewardess Gabriella.

In just a few minutes, Elise clapped her hands to get everyone's attention. She stood in center stage. Again, she wore black tights (she wore them well) and a bulky gray sweatshirt hanging atop the tights, sleeves pushed up to her elbows. She held a thick folio of the script in one hand. "Okay, you great actors, we're going to take a stab at going through the entire play, if we can. Whether we go all the way through tonight or not, we'll certainly get into it enough for you to get the feel of it and the pace that I want to set." She looked around at the cast members, each one in turn. "Okay," she said, "let's start with Bernard and Gloria finishing breakfast."

Lib and David Lynch stepped forward and began. Mary Ann stood back a couple of paces, preparing to enter when Bernard summoned her for more pancakes. Mary Ann knew her lines without referring to the script. It went well. The readings moved rapidly along. Elise only stopped the cast members infrequently with comments or suggestions as to how the lines should be delivered. After about forty minutes, Elise called for a short break. She smiled broadly. "You're all doing well," she said. She glanced at her watch. "I doubt if we'll get all the way through tonight. But we're making progress. Relax a couple of minutes and we'll pick up where we left off."

Mary Ann used the break to refer to the script and silently mouthed her upcoming lines. She was proud of how she was getting the lines without having to check the script as often as she thought she might. She took a couple of steps away from center stage, took a breath, and looked out at the few people who sat in the front row seats. Couple of boyfriends of the women players; one or two friends from the college perhaps, and the two "understudies" in case Pam or Valerie didn't make it.

Before Elise resumed the rehearsal, Mary Ann sidled over to Lib Owens, who sat on one of the fold-up chairs, staring off into the distance, her script in her lap. Mary Ann stood there a moment before saying, "I hope Thaddeus Sinclair and I didn't cut short your conversation with Chief Dalton yesterday."

Lib looked up, as if mildly startled. "Huh? Oh, no. We were just talking . . . and about finished anyway. Personnel thing, you know."

Mary Ann wanted to press a bit. "Everything okay? I hope it is."

"Oh, yes . . ." Lib's voice trailed off, and Mary Ann thought she might say something else, as if she wanted to but held back her words.

Elise gave a sharp clap of her hands. "Okay, players, let's get back with it. We'll start where Robert is astounded by Bernard's being able to shuffle the three stewardesses around in his life."

Phillip Mastik, playing Bernard's friend Robert, impressed Mary Ann with his—what?—flair for facial expressions and gestures. A perfect counter to playboy Bernard.

Elise nodded to Mary Ann to begin her lines as Berthe. Mary Ann muttered under her breath in French.

BERNARD: What's the matter now?
BERTHE: Nothing's the matter. I'm just doing my job,
         that's all. But now that America is gone, I've got
         to change the room for Italy.
BERNARD: She thinks of everything.

Elise chuckled. "Perfect, David and Mary Ann. Just the right tone. Love the facial expressions also." Elise bobbed her head. "Okay, proceed . . ." She turned to Phillip. As he came forward, Elise said, "You're doing great." He grinned and brushed back that blond streak of hair.

That night they got as far as the end of the first act before taking another break.

This time Mary Ann took one of the fold-up chairs. She realized she was a bit tired. Concentrating, trying to remember the lines—having to read them most of the time now—remembering the facial expressions and postures; it was hard work.

Lib came over and took the other chair beside Mary Ann. Mary Ann smiled and bobbed her head. "It's a lot to keep straight, isn't it?"

"Sure is." Once again Lib acted like she wanted to say something else. Mary Ann waited, but nothing came. Lib rubbed the palms of her hands together. Mary Ann waited again.

It was then, when Mary Ann casually glanced out at the auditorium, that she saw him. Officer Boyd Crocker sat unmoving on an aisle seat at the very back of the hall just beyond the entrance. She leaned closer to Lib. "You've got an admirer out there in the audience."

Lib looked surprised, maybe a bit pleased, and followed Mary Ann's gaze. But then Lib's face froze. Clearly, there was concern there. Her whole body seemed to stiffen. "Oh . . ." she uttered, the breath coming out of her as if she had been punched in the stomach. "It's Boyd . . ."

"I know," Mary Ann said. "Your former partner. Maybe he misses you."

Lib pretended to be studying the script that rested in her lap. Without looking up, she said softly, "Like I said, we don't work together." Then she risked a quick glance at Mary Ann. "That's what I was talking to the chief about yesterday. I asked to be relieved—from working with him."

Mary Ann didn't know what to say. So she kept quiet.

Lib stood, placed her script on the chair, and muttered, "I'm going backstage to the restroom . . . before we start again."

Mary Ann watched her leave. Then she glanced back out at the auditorium. Officer Boyd Crocker was not there. He had left.

Elise came forward to center stage; she clapped her hands. And rehearsal restarted. Mary Ann had several lines at the opening of Act II and she had to read from her script. She saw the slight frown on Elise's face when she finished and knew her lines sounded flat and uninspired.

From the corner of her eyes, she saw Lib come back on stage, standing at the back near where Jerry and Emma were quietly planning the next steps in building the set. Lib scanned the audience, holding her hands together in front of her. She breathed out, and from the relaxation of her shoulders, she seemed relieved she didn't see Boyd Crocker out there.

When rehearsal ended that night, Mary Ann tried to catch up with Lib Owens, who appeared ready to scurry away. But Lib paused a moment near the rear of the stage as Mary Ann approached her.

Lib brushed at her hair, smoothing it nicely even though it was not out of shape at all. "I ought to tell you something," Lib said. "You'll be hearing soon anyway." She rubbed her palms together, took a breath. "I'm leaving the force and taking a job as an officer with the Southern Shores police."

Mary Ann only said, "Oh . . ." Then, "But you'll still live here, and be in the play?"

"Yes, yes," Lib said. She tried to smile. "Southern Shores force is a better opportunity." Then she looked deeply into Mary Ann's face. "And I won't have to work with Boyd." She turned and left.

Mary Ann stood there; watched her go. She thought about how neat Lib's hair always looked. Mary Ann brushed the lock of her hair on the right side, the one that wouldn't lie like it was supposed to.

Most of the other cast members and their friends had left or were leaving. Elise said something about getting the lights. Mary Ann realized Elise was addressing Jerry and Emma, who with Tommy, had started moving set frames about. It was a big job, which meant Jerry would come home later, maybe much later.

Elise came up. "About ready to go?"

"Huh? Oh, yes . . ."

"Yeah?" Elise said.

"Yes, I was just thinking about Lib, and how upset she got when Officer Boyd Crocker sat there in the back, watching."

"I saw him," Elise said.

"Maybe sort of stalking her?"

"Maybe. Or maybe he wasn't even here to see her. Maybe he just wanted to see me in my tights." Elise chuckled.

Mary Ann smiled at Elise and shook her head. "You do look sexy in the tights."

"Yeah, I know I do." A big grin. She nudged Mary Ann and they exited the theater.

CHAPTER TWENTY-SEVEN

Saturday morning, Mary Ann let Jerry sleep. He had to go into work but not until late morning. Fairly early, she was up, showered, and dressed for story hour at the library. She wore tailored tan slacks, a long-sleeve cotton blouse, and boat shoes with socks. She had stepped out on the back porch to check the weather. Sunny and mild. Promised to be a nice day. It seemed to her that more than a week had elapsed since the last time she was there, but story hour had only been canceled the previous Saturday for Becky Thurston's funeral.

When she drove to the one-story brick library—one of the newest buildings in Camford Courthouse—Mary Ann saw a few cars already in the parking lot. One of those was the sparkling clean dark blue Lincoln Town Car that belonged to the library's benefactor, Justine Willis Gregory.

Mary Ann liked Justine Willis Gregory, and to Mary Ann's mild surprise, Justine seemed to really like her, and had a tendency to aim gentle teasing remarks her way from time to time, usually involving her working alongside Thaddeus Sinclair.

When she went into the library, Mary Ann saw Justine behind the counter in the small glassed-in office talking with head librarian Sue Wilson. They both stood tall facing each other. They were both about the same height, a half a head taller than Mary Ann.

Mary Ann raised a hand in greeting but didn't think either of them noticed her. She went on into the children's section to select a book to read to the children. Thinking of Becky's love

for birds, she chose a book about a robin and one about seagulls. Someone had already arranged a dozen small chairs in
front of the area where she would sit or stand to do her story
hour. Two small children—a boy and girl of about five or six—
were already seated and smiled at Mary Ann. She greeted them
and the one mother who stood at the back against the wall. In
just a few minutes, the other children and a few mothers would
arrive. Occasionally she got a husband or two also. The parents
must take turns attending.

Other children began to arrive. There were soon a total of
eight children and three more mothers. Most of the children
were pre-school, with first grade being the oldest. Then, just as
Mary Ann took her seat in a small chair at the front (she had to
sit on one hip, legs held out at an angle), a ninth child came in
holding his father's hand.

A few of the children Mary Ann recognized as regulars,
especially one rather stout young fellow who sat up front, as always. His round face beaming at Mary Ann. She smiled back at
him.

The children quieted when Mary Ann cleared her throat
and began. "Okay, boys and girls, today I thought I would read
to you from these two delightful books that . . ."

The little boy in front interrupted: "Tell us about Scootermonk instead. Please."

Two of the little girls chimed in. "Yes, please . . . please."

Mary Ann pursed her lips as if she were giving the request
careful consideration.

"And be sure to tell us what Scootermonk looks like."

Mary Ann blew out an exaggerated sigh. "Well, okay. But,
Charlie, you know his name is Skoodlemonk . . . not Scootermonk."

"I know," he chuckled. "I know. But tell us what he looks
like. I always like that."

She laid the two picture books on the floor beside her and
folded her hands primly in her lap. "Well," she said, "we should
never make fun of the way Skoodlemonk looks—we should

never make fun of the way anyone looks."

Two of the little girls nodded their heads in agreement.

"But tell us what Skoodlemonk looks like," Charlie said.

"Well, as you know, he has really big ears. I mean, really big and they stick out so it looks like he could use them to flap and fly with. And he has bright red hair that sticks up all over his head. No matter how much he tries to get it to lie down, it still sticks up."

Charlie laughed. "Sort of like your hair on the side?"

Two of the little girls giggled.

"We're not here to talk about *my* hair," Mary Ann said. But she smiled and patted at the lock of hair on the side; she saw two of the mothers in the back unconsciously touch their own hair, then drop their hands.

"Also," Mary Ann said, "he has a gap between his two front teeth, so when he talks real fast he makes a sort of whistling sound."

"And he could also spit," Charlie said.

"Yes, he could," Mary Ann said, "but he never did that in public because, as his mother said, it was impolite—not nice— to do that in public. So he did what his mother told him." She paused just a moment and scanned the children's rapt faces. "This day, Skoodlemonk decided to build an airplane. A real airplane that would be big enough to carry all of his friends for a ride."

The little boy behind Charlie said, "Wow."

"The airplane had big wings covered with silk that his mother gave him from scraps she had, and there were seats in the plane where his friends could sit. And of course he had seat-belts to make it safe." Mary Ann sat up straighter and shifted a bit in the tiny chair she perched on. "Now Skoodlemonk didn't want a gasoline engine in his airplane. In fact he didn't have a gasoline engine that would work. So you know what he did? He took seven hundred and fourteen rubber bands and tied them all together and hooked them up to the propeller so he could wind up the propeller and make his airplane fly just like you've seen small model airplanes fly with a rubber band motor. And now it was time for all of his friends to get in his red and yellow airplane with the silk wings and get ready to fly!"

The children all leaned forward in anticipation.

"So once everyone was in their seats and buckled up, Skoodlemonk called to his little friend Sallie Mae to pull the switch that would make the propeller start to turn. Now most of you remember Sallie Mae, don't you?"

Charlie said, "I do. She's little bitty."

"That's right. She's so small that most grown people—adults—can't even see her. You have to be one of Skoodlemonk's friends to see her. One or two of the mothers have thought they had seen Sallie Mae, but they couldn't be sure. One daddy said he was positive he had seen her, but no one was sure that he had."

One of the little girls mumbled, "I'll bet they couldn't really see her."

"Anyway, Sallie Mae sat up front right next to Skoodlemonk in the cockpit. She was his co-pilot. And she pulled the switch and the propeller started going faster and faster with all those seven hundred and fourteen rubber bands making it spin, faster and faster. Then the airplane began to roll forward, faster and faster, and pretty soon they were actually in the air! And all of his friends began to clap and say 'hooray' because they were flying over their houses and streets and everything. Some mothers and daddies came out in their front yards to see their children flying overhead in that bright yellow and red airplane that Skoodlemonk had made. All of his friends in the airplane waved and called to their mothers and daddies."

The children there in the library beamed and smiled as if they too were flying in the air over their parents' heads.

"Skoodlemonk thought that it would be fun if they flew down to the Outer Banks and out over the beach and ocean. Not far out over the ocean, but just a little ways so they could watch the surf and maybe see some porpoises swimming in the ocean. So, all of the children began to lean out the sides of the airplane to look down at the ocean and, sure enough, they did see three porpoises swimming along and jumping out of the water from time to time. And it looked like to Skoodlemonk's friends that the porpoises were waving at them and smiling because they—the children and the porpoises—were having so much fun."

Mary Ann got a very serious expression; the children's expressions mirrored hers. Without breaking stride with her story, Mary Ann noticed that Justine had joined the mothers at the back of the room.

"But then, just when they were having so much fun, you know what happened?"

"What?" several of the children said in unison.

"The propeller on the airplane stopped turning. All of the seven hundred and fourteen rubber bands had finally run all the way down. Skoodlemonk's friends stopped laughing and calling to the porpoises—because the bright yellow and red airplane didn't have any more motor. The rubber band motor had been used up, and very slowly at first, the airplane began to glide slowly down toward the ocean."

Mary Ann held one hand up and demonstrated how the airplane would slowly begin to descend. The children sitting before her had their mouths partly open, their eyes wide in anticipation of what would happen next.

"Skoodlemonk said, 'Uh-oh.' But little Sallie Mae said, 'Don't worry.' And what she did was whistle real loud. What she whistled was a tune, a song, that none of Skoodlemonk's friends—or even Skoodlemonk—had ever heard before. The song she whistled was really pretty. And it was loud. Then, while little Sallie Mae was whistling, the strangest thing began to happen. What happened was that seagulls—a lot of them—began to fly toward Sallie Mae and the airplane, which was getting closer and closer to the ocean." Mary Ann paused, and intoned ominously: "Closer and closer."

As a group, the children all leaned farther forward in their chairs. They didn't want to miss a word. Even Charlie was quiet, a worried look on his face.

"And the strangest thing happened then," Mary Ann said, her face lightening. "What happened is the seagulls—there must have been ten or fifteen of them—swooped down on the airplane and grabbed hold of the airplane's wings and began to lift it by flapping *their* wings. Then three big fat pelicans flew up and took hold of the tail of the airplane and began lifting it too so that the airplane was flying level. Skoodlemonk clapped his hands in joy, and little Sallie Mae kept on whistling that song, which the seagulls and the pelicans really liked. They were actually carrying the airplane—flying with it."

Charlie bobbed his head and said, "Oh, boy!"

"Skoodlemonk pointed toward home and the seagulls and the pelicans flew them right back home and set the plane down as gently as a feather, right where they had taken off. And all of Skoodlemonk's friends began to applaud and yell out 'Hooray!' The mothers and the fathers saw the seagulls and the pelicans bring the airplane home and they ran out there and hugged their children. Everyone was happy."

Mary Ann put her palms on her knees and spoke solemnly to her audience. "Skoodlemonk promised the mothers and the fathers that if they went up flying again in his airplane they wouldn't go so far . . . and that he would use even more than seven hundred and fourteen rubber bands. Then Skoodlemonk said, 'But what we all want to do is to thank Sallie Mae for whistling that song and calling the seagulls and the pelicans to help us.'"

Mary Ann stopped, her brow knitted. "But the parents said, 'Who is Sallie Mae?' Because they couldn't see her." Mary Ann shook her head. "And that's the way it is: Sometimes we grownups can't see the very person who helps us." She gave a conspiratorial wink. "But you children can."

Mary Ann took a deep breath and straightened her shoulders, signaling that story hour was over. The children—and their parents—applauded.

Mary Ann had to twist sideways to struggle up off of the little chair she had been perched on. She stood and flexed her back as Justine Willis Gregory came to her. She shook hands with Mary Ann.

"You are very talented, Mary Ann," Justine said, her tone like a benediction.

Two of the mothers also came forward and stood a couple of feet behind Justine. They thanked Mary Ann for the story and said they were amazed at her imagination.

"Thanks very much," Mary Ann said, "to all of you." She chuckled. "As for imagination, I do a lot of daydreaming."

One of the mother's said, "I was so sorry to hear about Becky's tragic . . . death."

Mary Ann nodded and tried a smile. "I know," she managed to say.

Justine said, "The birds, Mary Ann. A tribute to Becky? I know how fond she was of birds."

Again, Mary Ann nodded. She swallowed, and said, "I thought the birds would be appropriate."

After the mothers, smiling, left with their children, Justine said, "Speaking of daydreaming, how are you and Thaddeus getting along?" There was a mischievous twinkle in her eyes.

Despite herself, Mary Ann felt a blush creep across her face. "Now, Mrs. Gregory, he's my boss and an excellent writer and editor, but . . ."

"It's Justine, not Mrs. Gregory, as I've told you." She patted Mary Ann's forearm. "Love to tease you a bit, my dear." Then she cocked her head to one side. "Just the same, Thaddeus is very attractive man—in a scruffy sort of way." She pursed her lips. "Of course, he was married once—I think his ex-wife is in New York—but there are a lot of women in this town who would like to be working as closely with him as you are."

"Well, we work together. That's all."

"Um-huh," Justine said. She smiled again and turned to leave, stopped and looked back at Mary Ann. "More seriously, anything new on poor Becky Thurston's investigation? I know you and Thaddeus are working on that."

Mary Ann shifted her stance. "No, nothing new . . . and

that's a shame."

Justine nodded her head very slowly. "I do believe, how-ever, that something will break on the case before long. Some-thing like that can't go unsolved. Not in this town." She turned and left.

Softly, Mary Ann said, "Let us hope." *Something's just got to break before long. Or I'm going to make it break . . . and that's a promise, dear Becky.*

That night Jerry had another date with Emma, and Mary Ann stayed around the house. Close to nine o'clock she sat in the living room on the sofa and surfed TV channels with the sound muted. She heard a pickup truck drive slowly by and she thought at first it might be Jerry coming home early. The engine sounded a little too loud for Jerry's small truck. A few minutes later she heard the same motor rumble as the vehicle crept by her house. She thought for a moment that it was stopping in front of her house, but then it kept going, so very, very slowly.

She got up and locked the front door. When Jerry was out, she usually didn't bother with locking the front door, not until they went to bed.

She cut the living room lamps off and peered out the win-dow. The street was empty.

Maybe I'm just getting sort of spooked, paranoid.

She was determined not to dwell on it. So she went upstairs to bed, after turning one lamp back on as a welcome for her son when he returned.

CHAPTER TWENTY-EIGHT

Sunday morning just past seven the phone rang.

Mary Ann was still in bed and Jerry was probably asleep since he didn't get in until late. Mary Ann frowned at the phone on the bedside table. She checked caller ID. Saw that it was Thaddeus.

With a start, she sat up in bed and answered the phone as it began the second ring. Her voice was a bit thick from sleep, and she tried to make it sound better as she answered.

Thaddeus launched right in. "I know it's early. But I was sure you'd want to know." He took a quick breath. "We've got another homicide."

She was almost afraid to ask.

"Jamie Driscoll," Thaddeus said. "He was found about dawn this morning on the side of County Road 1157, southeast of town."

"Oh my . . ." was all Mary Ann could get out. *So much for expanding his business.*

"I'm going out there," Thaddeus said. "Thought you'd want to go with me."

"Yes . . . yes."

"I'll be by to pick you up in about ten or fifteen minutes, if you can make it by then."

"Yes . . . Let me throw something on."

"Bring your camera," he said.

Mary Ann was already out of bed as they signed off. She made a hurried trip to the bathroom, peeling off her old pajamas as she went. Brushed her teeth, splashed water on her face, shook her head at her hair, and thought about maybe a baseball cap. Within five minutes she was dressed in her slacks from yesterday, a lightweight, long-sleeve pullover top, sneakers without socks.

She stuck her head in Jerry's room. "There's been a homicide out in the country. Thaddeus is picking me up in about five minutes . . ."

Jerry roused himself on one elbow. "Who?"

"Jamie Driscoll. I don't think you know him."

She hurried downstairs. No time for coffee, but she'd start it anyway in case Thaddeus was fifteen minutes instead of the ten. She grabbed her camera and a tan windbreaker that originally had been Jerry's. A single cup of coffee was ready— ready enough to pour into a to-go cup and head out to the front porch to await Thaddeus.

The morning was cool and crisp, but the sun was out and it promised to be another beautiful fall day. She rested her coffee on the porch railing and slipped on the windbreaker.

She didn't have to wait long.

She heard Thaddeus's truck coming fast down Sycamore Street, and she grabbed her coffee and went hurriedly down the steps to the curb. He pulled up and she had the passenger side door open the instant the truck stopped. The camera was slung around her neck and she passed her to-go cup to Thaddeus to hold while she clambered up into the seat.

He nodded a "morning" at her and pushed the truck forward, faster than he normally drove. But there was no traffic this early on a Sunday morning.

Mary Ann took a sip from the cup, burning her tongue slightly. She wiped a drop of coffee from her chin. "Details?" she said.

"Know very little yet. We'll find out more. Dalton and others are at the scene. Body is still there." He glanced at the camera. "You should keep that camera out of sight when we first get there. When they get more comfortable with us, you'll be able to get some shots."

Mary Ann stared through the windshield. "Wonder what he was doing out there?"

"Maybe meeting a supplier? I don't know. Drug deal gone bad? I don't know."

Mary Ann swallowed. "How was he . . . how was he killed?"

"I'm not sure yet. I heard it on the police scanner, phoned Dalton. He was headed out. Only thing he said was didn't look like he had been shot." Thaddeus made a right turn at the edge of town, heading southeast.

He said, "Delivery person saw his vehicle, then the body off to the side of the road and called it in."

"Delivery person this early on Sunday morning?"

"I think it was one of the rural newspaper deliveries. Probably *The Virginian-Pilot*." With a wry half-chuckle, he said, "If it was the *Pilot*, he'll call his office and we'll likely have competition right away."

Mary Ann nodded and kept looking straight ahead. *A murder scene and the body's still there. Can't help but be nervous about that.*

Thaddeus glanced at her. "You okay?"

"Fine."

He took another quick look and then back at the two-lane country road. "Must say you look fine, Mary Ann . . . especially for having been roused out of bed early after a Saturday night."

Involuntarily, she patted at her hair. She'd forgotten the baseball cap. "Yeah, I'll bet I do," she said.

Another turn, this one to the left, and they were on County Road 1157. The area was definitely rural. Flat farm fields stretched out practically to the horizon, or at least to stands of pine trees a couple of acres in the distance. Stubble remained in many of the fields. Farmhouses were sparse and set back far from the road, usually with large trees around the houses to break the wind.

A mile or so further on and they made a gentle curve and

beyond the bend they saw flashing lights of an emergency vehicle, a state trooper's cruiser with the light bar flashing, and
several other cars, including a cruiser from the town and probably Chief Dalton's private car.

Mary Ann was already unbuckling her seatbelt when Thaddeus began to slow. *What in the hell was Jamie doing out here?
A customer at one of the farmhouses?*

They stopped at least twenty-five yards before the scene.
Thaddeus drove the outside wheels of his truck off the edge of
the road so he was in no way blocking passage. "Can you get
out over there okay?" he said to Mary Ann.

She took one more sip of the coffee, set the cup atop the
console, and nodded an affirmative at Thaddeus. She was careful getting out of the truck because there was a shallow ditch
just beyond the right wheels. Parched weeds grabbed at her
ankles. She wished she'd taken time to put on socks.

As Mary Ann and Thaddeus walked slowly to the scene,
she tucked her camera under the edge of her windbreaker. Getting closer to the activity, Mary Ann could hear the crackle of
police and emergency vehicle radios. Even in the sun, the flashing lights atop the vehicles were bright and, to Mary Ann,
vaguely disturbing.

To the side of the road, just off the pavement a couple of
feet, and near the front of what apparently was Jamie Driscoll's
truck, several officials, including Chief Dalton, stood over a
shrouded form. One person knelt at one end of the gray shroud
—what looked like a blanket of some sort—and lifted a corner.
Up closer still, Mary Ann could see the feet and part of a lower
leg at the other end of the blanket. She caught a glimpse of the
tattoo. And she felt a touch of nausea, a little dizzy. The coffee
didn't sit well on her empty stomach. It was like an acid burn. If
she'd investigated him further or followed him as she'd intended, maybe she could have saved him.

Or maybe she'd be dead too.

The person who had knelt near the head of the body slowly
stood and said something to Dalton. She recognized him as one

of the medical techs. Dalton nodded.

Officer Lib Owens, still looking fashionably petite in her uniform, stood in the middle of the road; she stepped back and waved a farmer's pickup on through. Mary Ann could see the driver peering at the scene, driving slowly on ahead. Mary Ann scanned the scene again. She didn't see Officer Boyd Crocker.

To Mary Ann, Thaddeus whispered, "Step back and get an overall shot of the vehicles and activity. Not the body."

Mary Ann nodded and retraced her steps. She shot several frames. Lib was visible in two of them standing off to one side. Despite what Thaddeus had said, she moved to the right and got an overall frame of three people standing around the form on the ground.

A fairly new Ford sedan pulled up close behind her and she stepped to the shoulder. The driver got out. He was a big man, about fifty, and he wore a jacket over dress slacks. He produced ID and flashed it at Lib and then went over and shook hands very briefly with Dalton. Thaddeus had come up close to Mary Ann as she moved back nearer the scene. "SBI agent from Elizabeth City," Thaddeus said.

Dalton, the SBI agent, and two others—a uniformed officer from Dalton's force whom Mary Ann had seen before but didn't know, and a different medical tech—conferred. Thaddeus had moved closer so he could hear what they were saying. Mary Ann stayed back a few feet. Dalton saw Thaddeus and gave a tiny bob of his head.

Then another car pulled up and parked behind Thaddeus's truck. The young man who got out was Jeff Hubbard, a reporter for *The Virginian Pilot* stationed in Elizabeth City. Mary Ann figured that a reporter for the *Daily Advance* of Elizabeth City would arrive before long.

With no more than a nod in Mary Ann's direction, Jeff Hubbard strode up to the officials standing near the body—and was promptly told to get back.

Mary Ann smiled about that. But the reporter hung back only a pace or two, notepad and pen at the ready.

*Oh, well, so much for an exclusive for the Camford Cour-
ier. But no way a weekly could compete on breaking news with
the dailies. Well, we'll just have to write better and tackle different angles.*

Mary Ann watched as the SBI agent, with latex gloves,
opened the driver's door of Jamie's truck, looked inside, felt
around on the seat and floorboard, and then went to the other
side, opened the passenger door, searched through the open
glove compartment. He pulled out several papers and a map.
Nothing else. She heard him say something to Dalton about im-
pounding the truck, having a forensic team go over it inch-by-
inch.

Mary Ann walked over to Lib Owens. Lib permitted a half-
smile and shook her head as if in disbelief.

"So much for a lovely Sunday morning, huh?" Mary Ann
said. She stood close to Lib, who scanned the road in both directions for any approaching cars.

Lib said, "Yeah." But her voice was pleasant, maybe a bit
guarded.

"Did you get out here first thing?" Mary Ann asked.

Lib nodded. "The chief called me and told me to come in
early—I was scheduled for seven anyway—and ride with him
over here. We were about the first ones here. Except for Officer
Bingham." She canted her head toward the uniformed officer
standing near the body.

Mary Ann shifted her stance, flexed her shoulders. "I
thought Officer Boyd Crocker would be here. He has night duty
. . ."

Without looking at Mary Ann, Lib said, "Sick leave. He
called in sick last night. About halfway through his shift."

Mary Ann raised her eyebrows. "He doesn't look like he's
ever been sick."

Lib looked at her, acted as though she was going to say
something, but remained silent.

Mary Ann said, "The body—Jamie Driscoll—you were
here early. How was he killed? I'd heard that he wasn't shot."

Lib took a breath. "He wasn't covered up when we got here." She shuddered. "But the way his head was turned. He'd been hit in the face, too, but his head . . . his head was turned at such an angle his neck had to be broken. That's what one of the medics said, too."

Mary Ann did her best to keep her face neutral. But her mind raced. *My God, and Becky's neck was almost broken. Same killer?*

She was sure of it.

CHAPTER TWENTY-NINE

It was almost nine that morning before the activity began to wind down. Chief Dalton and the SBI agent had given permission to the medics to go ahead and load Jamie's body into the rescue vehicle, head to Greenville where an autopsy would be performed. Mary Ann heard them talking about a broken neck, no other visible wounds other than a blow to the face that could have broken his nose; it was a hell of a hit on the face.

One of the medics estimated an unofficial time of death—based on the amount of rigor mortis—as sometime between midnight and two a.m. The call had come in from the rural newspaper carrier at close to six a.m.

Mary Ann watched as they loaded the body onto a gurney and then half-carried, half-rolled the gurney to the rear of the ambulance. The sight, which she had watched when Alan died, made her throat tighten. She had to look away, breathe deeply.

Lib stepped out onto the road and waved a sedan by. It carried an older couple, who twisted in their seats to try to see what was going on. Then she stopped another car to allow the ambulance to make a three-point turn on the two-lane road.

An area around Jamie's truck and where the body had lain remained encircled with crime scene yellow and black tape. Thaddeus and Dalton studied the ground from the edge of the road to where the body had been. Thaddeus pointed to weeds.

"It looks like he was dragged to the side of the road after he was killed," Mary Ann heard Thaddeus say.

The chief nodded in agreement.

Mary Ann started to walk over to where Lib stood. Five vehicles remained at the scene. Roof light bars on the Camford Courthouse police car continued flashing, as did those on the cruiser of a State Trooper. Then, with its white and yellow lights flashing, a tow truck came from the town area. Jamie's truck would be taken to an impoundment in Elizabeth City where the SBI forensic team could go over it.

While the tow truck got in place, Lib moved back into the road in case it was necessary for traffic control. Cables were attached, the mechanism engaged, and with a groan and grinding, the pickup was pulled aboard the tow. Another three-point turnaround, with Lib at the ready for any traffic, and the tow truck was gone. Thaddeus continued to chat with Dalton; *The Virginian-Pilot* reporter had managed to maneuver his way into the conversation.

Lib leaned against the side of the Camford Courthouse cruiser. She had been standing for at least two hours, and probably without any breakfast. Mary Ann realized she had missed hers too. She wasn't hungry. Just a bit weak, but her adrenaline was keeping her going. She sidled up to Lib and joined her beside the cruiser.

"Tired?"

Lib nodded, staring off across the road to a mostly barren field that had probably contained corn.

Mary Ann tried again. "Any theories as to who and why?"

Lib shook her head.

"Don't mean to pester you . . . and not playing reporter." Mary Ann tried something of a smile. "Just chatting."

Lib took a breath, her face now a little less vacant. "Sorry," she mumbled.

Then Lib said, "I've seen bad wrecks before, of course. But this is the first murder scene I've ever . . . ever worked."

"I've never seen one before, either. At least when the body, you know, when the body was still there and all." She paused. "And I'd seen that person, that victim—Jamie Driscoll—before."

Lib looked at her.

"I don't mean I knew him," she said hurriedly. "But I've seen him before." Then Mary Ann posed a question. "Drugs, you think?"

"Probably . . ."

Mary Ann thought Lib wanted to say more, but Lib let her voice trail off. Was it the cop in her that made her reluctant to talk, or was it something else? Maybe uncomfortable speculating with a reporter?

Out of the corner of her eye, Mary Ann saw Thaddeus leaving the chief and others, starting her way.

She figured it was time to go. She wanted to talk with Lib more. Maybe later. "See you at rehearsal Wednesday night?"

"Huh? Oh, yes, Wednesday night."

Mary Ann joined Thaddeus.

"Ready to go?" he said.

"Yes."

"We've got to get you something to eat. Breakfast. Me too."

"I'm really not hungry."

"You've got to eat."

"Well, yes. Okay."

They got in the cab of his truck, and Mary Ann was careful not to knock over her to-go coffee. She held it in one hand and took a sip of the cold coffee. Her mouth was dry.

They drove away.

They were quiet.

Then Thaddeus said, "Bunny's has a nice brunch on Sunday mornings."

"Okay." Her voice was flat.

Thaddeus glanced at her. Back at the road. Didn't say anything.

Mary Ann stared straight ahead, holding the coffee cup in her left hand. "Why had he stopped right there in the middle of nowhere?"

"I don't know. Meeting another dealer? And something

went wrong?"

Mary Ann was quiet for maybe a quarter of a mile on the lonely two-lane road. "Seems like a strange place to meet someone."

Another quick glance from Thaddeus. "What are you thinking?"

"Oh, I don't know. But maybe somebody made him stop."

They were mostly quiet then until they got into town and Thaddeus parked in the side lot beside Bunny's Restaurant. As they passed a vent on the side of the building, Mary Ann smelled the heavy cooking aroma and grimaced.

Thaddeus caught the look. "You've got to eat something."

"I know," she said. She patted at her hair, tried to straighten her top out, couldn't decide whether to tuck it in or leave it hanging outside. "I don't look much like the church crowd," she mumbled.

"We're near the beach. Casual," Thaddeus said. "And you look fine." He smiled at her. "You always do . . . even when I rouse you out of bed to go to a murder scene."

"Yeah, right," she said, and they went inside.

Most of the tables and a few of the booths were occupied. Many of the customers were in Sunday clothes. But Mary Ann was relieved to see a few people in jeans and casual shirts. Over to one side, in a table by the window, she saw Justine Willis Gregory sitting with two other women about her age. They were dressed elegantly.

Justine saw Mary Ann and Thaddeus. As Bunny led the two of them to a vacant table at the back, Justine gave Mary Ann a nice smile, a knowing smile, a twinkle in her eyes.

No, no, it's not what you think. We've been at a murder scene. He's my boss, my editor. That's all. There's nothing to it, no matter what you think.

But Mary Ann returned Justine's smile. *Well, I am pleased to be here with Thaddeus. I do like him, admire him.*

The same waitress they had before approached them. To Thaddeus, she said with a smile, "Don't tell me you want your usual."

"Not this morning," he said. "I'll have the three-egg omelet, American cheese and ham. Orange juice."

"Coffee? Both of you?"

"Please."

The waitress turned to Mary Ann. "Just one egg, over light.
Whole-wheat toast. Bacon. Ice water with lemon. Please."

The waitress nodded and returned with the coffee pot. Mary
Ann wasn't sure whether she should try more coffee, but she
did take a tentative sip. It actually tasted good to her.

"A trip to the restroom," she said.

"Me, too," he said. He grinned, "For one thing, want to
wash my hands thoroughly. You feel that way after you've been
to a scene like that."

"Yes," Mary Ann said, with a vigorous nod of her head.

When they came back to the table and waited for their food,
Mary Ann studied her flatware, straightening the fork, lining up
the spoon with the knife.

"What are you thinking?" Thaddeus said.

Mary Ann exhaled and looked up at Thaddeus. "Well, I
keep imagining the scene out there. I mean before . . . in the beginning. Why Jamie stopped there in the country, no one
around. What would make him stop?"

"Yes?" Thaddeus watched her steadily.

"Well, I mean the only way I would have stopped would be
if I were meeting someone, and that's a heck of remote area to
be meeting someone, even for a drug deal. There weren't any
identifying landmarks around. Or if someone was lying in the
road, like they knew I was coming and when to set it up. Or if
. . . if a police officer made me stop." Her chin up, she peered at
Thaddeus.

He lowered his head, then looked at her over the tops of his
little round glasses. "Be careful, Mary Ann. Careful what you're
thinking . . . and certainly what you're saying."

The waitress brought their food. She placed Thaddeus's
plate first, along with a stack of toast between them. Part of the

toast order was probably whole-wheat. It was difficult to tell. She set down Mary Ann's lone egg and two strips of bacon.

Thaddeus cut off a chunk of his steaming omelet, eased it into his mouth, and began chewing. He continued to eye Mary Ann. She busied herself with a small bit of bacon and a sliver of egg. She reached for a piece of toast, cut diagonally and buttered, although they hadn't asked for butter. She took another sip of coffee and a swallow of the ice water. She drank some more of the water.

Without any preliminary because Thaddeus was waiting, she said, "Officer Boyd Crocker was working last night until after midnight and then radioed in sick. That other officer who was there—Bingham or something—filled in for him the rest of his shift." She kept that chin up. "And Boyd Crocker was working the night Becky Thurston was killed."

Thaddeus shook his head. "Careful, Mary Ann. Careful."

"Well, he's certainly big enough and strong enough . . . and there's something about him that worries Officer Lib Owens. She doesn't want to work with him any more . . . and he was there watching her the other night at rehearsal . . . and in fact she's moving on to Southern Shores police department. Getting away from Boyd Crocker." Her words tumbled out fast, but she did remember to keep her voice down very low.

Thaddeus went back to his omelet, quietly thinking, pretending great interest in how he cut the omelet into bite-size sections. He wasn't eating as much as he was rearranging his food.

Maybe I shouldn't have said so much. Run my mouth. Thaddeus probably thinks I'm just being an emotional female. Speculating. But, heck, I'm a reporter . . . and . . .

Now Thaddeus laid down his knife and fork. "Mary Ann, the only thing I'm saying is be careful what you say. You can say it to me, but . . ."

"You're the only one I've said anything to." She knew she sounded testy. "Didn't mean to sound . . . that way," she said.

He continued. "I appreciate that it's just you and me talking." That warm smile was present. "You've got a great ability to put pieces of a puzzle together. And maybe it sounds like I'm also giving myself a pat on the back, but what you're saying has crossed my mind, too."

His expression was soft, and to Mary Ann it was endearing.

"This is between us, and I'm just saying, Mary Ann, be careful. Please."

Mary Ann felt like she might get tears in her eyes. *Well, I'm overly tired maybe.* "Thank you, Thaddeus." She nodded. "That means a lot to me." Quickly she looked down at her half-eaten egg.

When they got ready to go, Mary Ann glanced over to see that Justine continued to chat away with her women friends.

Thaddeus said, "I've got this."

But Mary Ann wanted Justine to see her paying something. "I'll get my part. I insist." She pulled out a five and a one.

"That's enough," Thaddeus said.

"You sure?"

He nodded. He added his cash to the check.

She took one more sip of her coffee, chased with another swallow of ice water. "Thaddeus, where did Boyd Crocker work before he came here?"

He pulled out two more ones. "Salisbury, North Carolina."

Mary Ann brightened. "Really? No kidding. I've got a friend from college who works for the city there. Register of deeds office. Karen. We still stay in touch. Social media kind of thing."

Thaddeus had stood. He stopped and looked at her. "Be careful, Mary Ann," he said again. "Be careful, please."

CHAPTER THIRTY

Thaddeus drove Mary Ann to her house. Jerry's truck was gone. A shift today at Food Lion. Before she got out, Thaddeus said, "I know what you're thinking about concerning your friend in Salisbury."

"I'll be very discreet . . . and she will too, I'm sure."

"Go take a nap," he said.

"I can use one. And probably look it, too."

"You look fine, Ace."

She smiled at him. It seemed the most natural thing in the world that she would give him a kiss goodbye. She resisted that impulse, though, but just the same reached over and patted his forearm. "In the morning," she said.

As she entered her front door, the telephone was ringing. She hurried to the set in the living room. It was Elise. Uh-oh.

"Oh, my God," Elise said. "I just heard on the news that Jamie Driscoll was murdered out in the country. Had you heard? Is that true?"

Mary Ann went into detail with what she knew and where she had been.

When Mary Ann finished, Elise was quiet for a moment. Her voice was breathy as she said, "Tell you the truth, that scares me. I mean, that killer is still out there somewhere."

"I know," Mary Ann said.

They talked for several more minutes. Before they signed off, Elise sounded a bit calmer. "See you Wednesday night . . . Berthe," she said.

Mary Ann sat there in the living room for a while longer, then went upstairs to her bedroom. She looked at herself in the mirror, shook her head. She slipped out of the slacks she wore to the scene, kept the top on, and climbed on the unmade bed and covered up lightly. She didn't think she would be able to fall asleep, but in just a few minutes she did. When she waked an hour and a half later, she felt groggy and out of sorts. Naps did that to her sometimes.

She got in the shower and ran the water as hot as she could stand.

On Monday, Chief Dalton agreed to have a press conference at eleven. Thaddeus and Mary Ann got there shortly before the briefing was scheduled. Three other reporters were already there, as well as the TV anchor and a newscaster from one of the radio stations. The chief came in wearing his uniform and a tie. Lib Owens followed him into the room. They both looked tired, although the chief tried to smile at the group. Lib stood to his side and slightly behind him as the chief placed a single sheet of paper on the podium.

Dalton opened the conference with a brief statement of what they knew, which was damn little except that James Driscoll had been found apparently slain; a homicide; his body on the shoulder of County Road 1157, southeast of town. A very rural area. When he finished, the questions came flying at him.

No, we have no arrests, no suspects.

No, we do not know what the motive was.

No, we're awaiting an autopsy to determine exactly how he was killed, but we're sure it was a homicide.

No, he was not shot, nor stabbed. Preliminarily it looks more like a physical attack. But as I said, we're awaiting an autopsy report.

No, we don't know that drugs were involved.

No, we're not making any speculation of a connection between this homicide and that of Becky Thurston.

The questions began to dwindle down, and the chief signaled an end to the briefing and turned to leave.

By and large, it went as well as Mary Ann figured it could. She knew that Thaddeus wanted to catch up with Dalton, have a little sit-down with him. She planned to go back to the office by herself, leave Thaddeus here at the station. He'd have a better chance of chatting privately with Dalton with her not around.

The reporters shuffled out of the room, talking to each other. The TV anchor's cameraman folded up his equipment.

Mary Ann moved forward as Lib pushed the podium back against the wall and straightened a couple of the chairs.

Lib nodded at Mary Ann.

"You're doing double-duty," Mary Ann said, trying to make her voice sound upbeat.

Lib made a little puff sound, stood straighter. "I think we all are. Small force, anyway."

"I take it Boyd Crocker is still sick?"

Lib did a quick glance at Mary Ann. "Yes." Nothing else.

Mary Ann wanted her to say more, and she resisted an urge to push Lib a bit. Instead she said, "See you at rehearsal Wednesday night."

"Sure," Lib said, and managed a smile. It was obvious she was finished in the briefing room.

"I'll let you get back to work," Mary Ann said, and started to the rear of the room to exit. Lib nodded and headed out the other end of the room.

Back at the newspaper, Ethel spoke to Mary Ann as she came in. "I've got some leftover chicken potpie I made yesterday. You want some for lunch?"

"Well, that's awfully nice of you, Ethel. Why yes, that would be wonderful."

"In the fridge," Ethel said. "Let me get you some." She pried herself up from the desk and Mary Ann followed her into the tiny room next to her desk. The room had been a darkroom back before digital cameras and they had turned it into something of a luncheon area and semi-kitchen, complete with sink, small refrigerator and microwave. Ethel dished out a hefty portion of the chicken potpie onto a glass plate.

"Oh, that's plenty," Mary Ann said. "Thank you so much." She popped it into the microwave and Ethel hobbled back to her desk, favoring those ankles.

Mary Ann took the steaming potpie back to her desk and ate there while checking emails and other items that might have come in on her computer. The potpie was delicious. The crust was even still crisp. She looked at her notes taken at the press briefing and planned to write a few paragraphs that she would give to Thaddeus for inclusion in his main story on the killing of Jamie Driscoll.

When she had finished her lunch, she took the plate to the little room, rinsed it, set it aside to dry, and went back to her desk and scanned for her friend Karen's phone number in Salisbury. She made the call.

She was surprised to get Karen right away. After a preliminary exchange of so-good-to-hear-from-you, Mary Ann launched into her spiel about Boyd Crocker. But the way she told it, she made it sound as if she was doing a feature story about him and just wanted to gather a bit of background, including why he left Salisbury. "And, Karen, this is sort of a surprise because Boyd doesn't know I'm doing a story, so please let's be discreet about it."

Karen agreed to do some checking and promised to phone Mary Ann back shortly.

When they hung up, Mary Ann felt vaguely uneasy. She didn't like the subterfuge she engaged in with Karen. But she put it out of her mind to get a few paragraphs written for Thaddeus.

Mary Ann was just finishing a summary of the press briefing when Thaddeus came into the paper. She heard him speak to Ethel, who had a couple of messages for him, and offered him some pot pie, which he said he certainly appreciated and would come back in a few minutes and take advantage of it. He started toward his office, but stopped and stuck his head into Mary

Ann's office. She told him she had a few paragraphs that she was just finishing about the briefing.

"Good," he said. "Send them back to me. I'll work them into the story, or maybe as a sidebar."

"Let me finish editing and I'll shoot them to you." Then, "How did it go with Chief Dalton? Get to see him?"

Thaddeus sighed and stepped inside the office. He pulled one of the extra chairs on its rollers over closer to Mary Ann. "Yep I talked with him, but . . ."

"But what?"

"He was really distracted about something. I asked him what was worrying him. He said, 'You mean beside the fact that we've got a second homicide that's unsolved?' But I told him I thought it was something else, too." Thaddeus paused, looking down at his folded hands.

Mary Ann said, "Well, that's enough for him to be sort of . . . sort of distracted."

"Um-huh. But it was more than that. I mean I know that's enough, but it was something else. Something he didn't want to talk about. I sensed that. He said, 'Oh, personnel matters, I guess.' Then he mentioned that Lib Owens was leaving the force and going with the Southern Shores department."

"That's personnel, all right," Mary Ann said.

Thaddeus rose. "Something else," he said. "It was something else." He shook his head and started to his own office. "Don't know what."

Mary Ann went back to reading through the paragraphs she had written, making a few edits.

And she got a call back from Karen in Salisbury.

CHAPTER THIRTY-ONE

The first thing Karen said was, "Maybe it's not such a good idea to be doing a feature story on Boyd Crocker."

"Why is that?"

Karen paused a moment, then spoke softly, guardedly, as if she held a palm partially over mouthpiece. "I'd heard some rumors about him when he left. Something about some stuff he had confiscated during an arrest—stuff that went missing."

"Drugs?"

"I think so. But I don't know." She paused again. "And he got in trouble at least once, I heard, for beating up a suspect. Put the guy in the hospital." Another moment or two of silence. "You told me to be discreet, and I was." She paused again. "But I did speak to a lieutenant, a guy I dated for a while before Ken and I got married, and we're still friends, and I asked him about Boyd. Told him a reporter was doing a story on him. Tell you the truth, he got a little upset. You know how cops are—they look after each other."

Mary Ann kept quiet.

Karen said, "I hope I didn't screw up anything by speaking . . . speaking to the lieutenant." Another pause. "As I said, maybe you'd better do your story from at your end, and forget Salisbury. Oh, and Boyd was not fired exactly but he was allowed to resign."

When they ended their conversation, Mary Ann sat for several minutes just looking at the telephone and thinking. *I've got to tell Thaddeus, but I don't want to. Well, I've got to.*

She delayed going into Thaddeus's office as long as she could. Gene entered and loped around to his desk, speaking briefly to Mary Ann, who remained seated at her desk. Gene smelled like French fries and hamburgers. He carried a large plastic cup in his hand, obviously left over from his late lunch.

Mary Ann rose, exhaled a deep breath and headed to Thaddeus's office. He faced his computer screen but looked up at Mary Ann over the tops of his glasses. "Yes?"

She took the seat in front of his desk. An empty plate that had contained a portion of pot pie was pushed to one side. She launched right in without taking any more time to debate with herself about the conversation with Karen. "I called my friend in Salisbury, and sort of finessed around that I was doing a feature story on Boyd Crocker."

Thaddeus rested his forearms on the edge of his desk.

Mary Ann wasn't sure whether that was the beginning of a frown on his face.

"Well, she called back . . ." Mary Ann shifted in her chair. "First thing she said was maybe I shouldn't be doing a story about Boyd Crocker." Then Mary Ann went into detail about the missing evidence apparently confiscated following an arrest, and Crocker's beating up a suspect, and how, while he wasn't fired, he was permitted to resign. She hesitated, and then also told Thaddeus that Karen's lieutenant friend seemed a little upset with her. But that she had tried to be discreet.

Thaddeus didn't say anything for a minute, two minutes. Mary Ann waited; she kept her eyes trained on his face, which was turned downward. He looked up at Mary Ann. "If Boyd's still got some friends on the force in Salisbury, he'll hear about the phone call."

Mary Ann swallowed. She shook her head. "Maybe I shouldn't have made the call?"

"No, it needed to be made." He took his glasses off, one of the few times Mary Ann had ever seen him do that, and he rubbed the heels of both hands on his eyes. *He doesn't look quiet as much like a rumpled skeptic with his glasses off. But*

I'm used to him with his John Lennon glasses. They suit him.

Although he had certainly not reprimanded her, Mary Ann felt as though she had stepped beyond where she should have. "I know, I know, Thaddeus, you told me to be careful." She rubbed her hands together. "I'm not sure I have been that careful."

He nodded but kept silent. Then he looked right into her eyes, and said, "You think Boyd is a suspect?"

She shifted in the chair again as if she couldn't get comfortable. "Well, I don't know, Thaddeus, but Jamie Driscoll stopped way out there in the middle of nowhere, and I wonder who would get him to stop like that—a policeman would." She took a deep breath and exhaled. "Officer Boyd Crocker was on duty the night Becky was killed and on duty Saturday night." She held her chin up.

"He called in sick that night," Thaddeus said.

"Yes, but that wasn't until his shift was half over . . . after midnight, about when Driscoll was killed." She jabbed at the air for emphasis. "And Lib Owens doesn't want to work with him. She's not saying all that is on her mind. I know that. But there's something about him that Lib, a fellow officer who was his partner, doesn't like."

"She hasn't come right out and said that, has she?" Thaddeus said.

"Well, no, she hasn't. It's more like what she won't say." Mary Ann knew it all sounded pretty weak. She added, "And he's certainly big enough and strong enough to have killed Becky and Jamie Driscoll." She sank back in her chair.

Thaddeus was quiet. "So are a number of people . . . including your fellow actor David Lynch."

Mary Ann nodded. *Playing devil's advocate a bit here, Thaddeus?*

Thaddeus's intercom buzzed. Ethel's voice: "You've got a call from Chief Dalton, line one."

Thaddeus raised a hand to Mary Ann to keep her seat. "Yes, Chief," Dalton said. He listened for a minute, two minutes. "Thanks very much for the update," Thaddeus said and put the phone back in its cradle.

He looked at Mary Ann. "Medical examiner confirms that Driscoll's neck was broken, causing his death. He also was hit hard in the face and even harder in the stomach."

Mary Ann was silent.

Thaddeus took a breath. "Also, preliminary from SBI forensic team in Elizabeth City, Driscoll's truck was wiped clean. Hardly any fingerprints, even of Driscoll's. No drugs found."

Her chin forward, Mary Ann said, "Any drugs—and there would have been some if he was delivering—were stolen, just like at Becky's."

Thaddeus nodded. "Yes." He waited a moment, then said, "They're not through with the body yet. A bit of skin found under the fingernails of the right hand. Maybe defensive. But maybe the skin is his own. It'll take a while to sort that out. Any DNA can take weeks. Not like on TV."

Mary Ann said, "Well, it's nice of the chief to let you know."

"Yes it is. He needs someone to talk to." Thaddeus shook his head. "To tell the truth, I feel a little sorry for him. He's doing his best and I know he's getting a lot of pressure. I mean, two violent homicides right here together and in this small town where not that much violent happens."

Gene stuck his head in the office door. Apparently, he had heard part of the last conversation. He chuckled and said, "Nothing much violent here unless you count cross words among the school board members—where I'll be tonight."

Thaddeus and Mary Ann both smiled. *Well, a little levity, even from Gene, is welcome at this point.*

CHAPTER THIRTY-TWO

Wednesday evening, as Mary Ann drove to the Tracks Community Theater, she couldn't help but continue thinking of how no progress at all had been made in solving either the Becky Thurston or Jamie Driscoll killings. A real standstill. Even after several more conversations between Thaddeus and Chief Dalton, nothing had developed. Nothing. Nada. Yet, she had more than just a gut feeling that Boyd Crocker could possibly—just possibly—be a real suspect.

Thaddeus had referred more than once to how Chief Dalton appeared distracted, and how he kept avoiding what really concerned him, always attributing it to "personnel concerns" and paperwork.

If it were really personnel concerns, what were these—other than the fact he'd have to get a replacement for Officer Lib Owens? Lib would be making her move to Southern Shores any day now.

Could it be Boyd Crocker? Dalton never once even mentioned Crocker's name. As far as Mary Ann knew, he was still on sick leave. He was not at the fitness center Monday evening when Mary Ann went there. Neither was Lib, but she didn't expect her there any longer because of her upcoming move.

Mary Ann pulled into the parking area of the theater and surveyed the vehicles that were already there. She saw Jerry's little truck and a big Ford 150 pickup that she assumed was Tommy's. Jerry, Emma, and Tommy had arrived earlier that afternoon to work on the set. Mary Ann parked near Elise's

Mustang, giving enough room so her door would not ding Elise's pride and joy. Three other cars were there. She checked her watch. Not late, but maybe everyone else had just come extra early.

She entered through the stage door, her favorite place, took a deep breath as always to smell the theatrical aroma. Also, this time there was a mixture of freshly sawed lumber. The set was all but finished. Painting still had to be done. Three doors were in place (one for each of the stewardesses' bedrooms), a fake window at the back, a small dining table, a sofa, end table and telephone on a slender table.

Elise talked with Pam, Valerie, and Lib, apparently giving them last minute instructions before starting the rehearsal. Tonight, Elise wore a tight-fitting top and slender jeans. Her figure on display. Pam and Valerie were dressed much more casually. Well, almost workout-scruffy. Lib had come from duty and was still in part of her uniform, minus the heavy belt with her sidearm, handcuffs, and other paraphernalia, which she had probably stowed just off stage.

David Lynch and Phillip Mastik stood to one side chatting with each other. Phillip laughed at something David said. He always threw his head back when he laughed and at the same time brushed the lock of peroxide blonde hair back one-handed.

Elise stepped to center stage, clapped her hands together and said, "Let's take it from the top." She then blocked out the opening scene, telling the players where they were supposed to be.

Mary Ann took her place off stage right so she could enter from the not-visible "kitchen." Lib and David Lynch sat at the small dining table finishing breakfast.

Elise went down front and took a seat on the front row. "Okay, the curtain goes up," she called out.

The rehearsal started.

As the action progressed, Elise stopped the players only a few times to make suggestions or correct something she didn't like. She had to prompt lines fairly frequently. Mary Ann delivered hers almost perfectly, and she was proud of that.

During one of the breaks, Elise came back on stage to confer with Pam and Valerie. David and Lib stood off to one side chatting with each other. Mary Ann watched them. At one point, he reached out and touched Lib briefly on the shoulder; they both smiled about something. *A burgeoning backstage romance? Well, it's happened before. I guess the world does really move on . . . after the finality of a death.*

Jerry came up to his mother. "We're finished up for tonight," he said. "Tommy's already gone. Emma and I are going to go get something to eat. I'll see you at home later." He turned to leave. "Oh, the play's going well. And you're not so bad yourself, Mom."

"Thanks. It's fun. I'm enjoying the role." Then, "You two be careful."

Rehearsal resumed when Elise went down front again.

By nine-thirty, it was beginning to wind down. The players were winding down, too. Mary Ann noticed that during short breaks, the players had a tendency to flop down on the nearest chair, or on the set's sofa. But they did manage to get all the way through the play, with the last scene with Bernard and Robert there alone . . . with a happy resolution with the three stewardesses.

It was then close to ten.

Elise said, "I know it's been a long rehearsal, but you are all doing great, and I certainly appreciate it. Friday night's rehearsal should go quicker now that we've ironed out some spots.

Without much chatter, the players began to put on sweaters or windbreakers in preparation for leaving. Valerie had come to rehearsal alone. Her husband was babysitting with their little one; Pam's boyfriend greeted her down front. Phillip waved a goodbye and he left too.

The only ones remaining were Elise, Mary Ann, David Lynch, and Lib. They stood talking in a loose grouping.

Lib faced backstage left. The door to the parking lot was a

few feet beyond the heavy purple side curtain. Elise had just said something to David when Lib's eyes grew wide. She sucked in her breath and made a soft moan, her gaze fixed on something beyond the edge of the curtain.

CHAPTER THIRTY-THREE

Boyd Crocker had pushed aside the curtain and stood there tall and glaring at Lib.

It was his eyes. The first thing Mary Ann noticed. That, and the way he was dressed. His overall appearance. He was not in uniform. A tight-fitting black T-shirt, black workout pants. His short hair didn't appear to have been combed in days. But his eyes. They were wide open, glassy, and as wild looking as those of an untamed and frightened horse on the prairie.

A long red scratch, a whelp, marred his left cheek, from above his cheekbone down to his chin.

His voice was raspy, filled with venom when he hissed out words to Lib: "You've been checking on me. Calling headquarters in Salisbury. Prying. Trying to pin something on me. I had you figured for a bitch, but I didn't know how much of one . . ."

Lib spoke out, her voice carrying well but with a tone of pleading in it. "I haven't called anybody about you, Boyd. No one."

He took a step toward them.

"You lying bitch. I got a call from someone still on the force that you phoned, pretending to be a reporter or something."

Mary Ann knew she had to say something. Defuse the situation. "It was me, Officer Crocker. I'm the one who called . . . doing a feature on you."

Crocker wheeled to face Mary Ann. He staggered slightly when he turned. "You're trying to cover for her." He lolled his head toward Lib. "In it together."

Lib, taking on her cop voice, said, "You're high, Boyd. You're high. Calm down and go home."

David Lynch edged closer to Lib. Elise had retreated a few steps and Mary Ann saw from the corner of her eye that Elise had her cell phone close to her face. Mary Ann hoped she had called 911. *Call 911, Elise. Please, for God's sake, 911.*

Mary Ann summoned bravado she didn't know she had. She made herself as tall as she could, her chin up; but her legs trembled. "You're high on those pills you stole from Becky Thurston and Jamie Driscoll."

A tremor, a wobbling, overtook his head, like he didn't have control of his neck muscles. Crocker said, "You're trying to pin it on me." Then he yelled out, taking in Lib, Mary Ann: "All of you. Trying to accuse me. Well you don't have a damn thing on me. Not a goddamn thing." He took another step toward them, his gait unsteady.

Mary Ann stood her ground. "Yes, we do, Boyd. We've got that DNA. Your skin under Jamie Driscoll's fingernails." They didn't yet have any DNA results, but she thought maybe she could make him believe it. "And you beat Becky Thurston to death when you knew she was going to end it with you and your drugs . . . and then you stole her medicines. And you killed Jamie Driscoll because—probably because he wanted to start moving in on your drug territory."

His eyes narrowed and his face pinched together in a horrid mask of rage. "You bitch," he growled.

Mary Ann steeled herself not to move back. She trembled all over, but she tried to make it not so apparent. She did her best to swallow, but her throat felt frozen.

Boyd Crocker's gray eyes burned with rage. His body tensed.

But David Lynch stepped between them. "Cool it, Boyd."

Boyd stopped, his upper lip curled in a sneer.

David stood poised on the balls of his feet, his arms down by his sides. "Just leave, Boyd. You're in no shape to be here."

David's voice was low and even, not threatening but firm and purposeful.

"Who the hell you think you are, pussy boy?" Boyd's head continued to wobble; the taunting smirk frozen on his face. Evil, belligerent. "I can take you down with one swipe of my hand."

"I don't think so, Boyd." Again, said evenly, matter of fact.

"Yeah?" Boyd's total attention now focused on David. "We'll just see . . ." He lunged toward David.

It was so fast that Mary Ann could hardly see more than a blur. David's right foot came up in a kick. He appeared to bounce as he kicked. The toe of David's shoe crushed into Boyd's groin.

Boyd let out a groan, like an animal, and he buckled over, shoulders hunched forward, his head the same height as David's waist.

Twisting his body, David's right elbow came up and he swung his upper torso, the elbow leading the way, and the elbow caught Boyd in the right temple. It sounded loud, bone on bone. Boyd's knees began to give away.

David's left hand swung with his whole body into the side of Boyd's throat. Boyd coughed and went down on his knees. David's right foot came up again and smashed into Boyd's chin. His head snapped back.

Boyd crumpled to the floor.

David kicked him again in the side of the head.

Lib rushed forward from the curtain at the rear of the stage. She had her handcuffs in one hand, her Glock service pistol in the other. "Enough, David," she yelled. "Move."

Lib came down on Boyd's back with her knees. She stuffed her pistol in the back of her pants. She grabbed one outstretched arm of Boyd's, snapping the cuffs on it, grabbing for the other arm, trying to bring them together behind Boyd's back. She had trouble with the maneuver. He lay there coughing, gasping for breath.

She looked tiny perched on Boyd's back. But he was no match for her—or David—at this point.

At first.

CHAPTER THIRTY-FOUR

Boyd made that animal growl again as Lib struggled to get his other arm cuffed. Suddenly Boyd pushed up with his arms and knees so hard he seemed to levitate off the stage floor. As he did so, he tossed Lib off his back like she was a rag doll.

Lib flipped over to Boyd's side, landing on her stomach.

David started forward.

But Boyd quickly darted his left arm around, snatching the pistol stuck in the back of Lib's waistband. The end of the cuff smacked against the back of Lib's head.

The Glock pistol in his hand, Boyd aimed dead center at David's chest.

David froze in his steps.

"Get the hell back," Boyd said, his voice choked and his words slurred.

Lib rolled over and scrambled to her feet.

Boyd, half-standing, kept them all at bay as he swung the pistol back and forth, glaring at each of them in turn. He shifted the pistol to his right hand. The arm with the cuff attached hung by his side.

Lib stepped back a step. She rubbed the back of her head where the end of the cuffs had smacked against her. She kept her head toward Boyd, but her eyes darted left and right, as if searching for a solution.

Mary Ann stood perfectly still, trying the keep her legs from trembling. Elise stood with her arms holding her chest, her eyes wide and frightened.

Lib, her voice sounding strained as if it took all the control she had to make it even, said, "Boyd, it's all over. You know that. There's no way out for you. You can't shoot us all. Put the gun down and . . ."

"Shut up. Shut the hell up." That animal growl.

Boyd looked around, then back at the four of them. He seemed confused. It was like he couldn't decide what to do. He tried to take a deep breath, but hunched over at the waist. Something hurt too much.

Lib tried again. "Boyd, please, there's no way . . ."

"I said shut up. Keep that bitch mouth shut." Then he mumbled, "I've got to think." His head wobbled. He shook his head, forcing himself to concentrate.

Mary Ann saw David tense as if he might make another lunge at Boyd. *Please don't, David. He'll shoot you—and the rest of us.*

They stood still, waiting for what would come next. And dreading it.

Then footsteps backstage. The purple curtain pushed aside and there stood Chief Dalton, a pistol drawn. Beside him, looking frightened, was young Officer Bingham. He held his weapon in both hands, his eyes wide. His hands shook.

Mary Ann realized she had hardly been breathing. *Thank God that was the call Elise made.*

"Put it down, Crocker," Chief Dalton said. "Just put it down. It's all over now."

Boyd Crocker moved to the side so he could see the chief and Bingham and still keep Mary Ann and the others in his line of vision. He bit on his lips, his head going back and forth.

"We've been to your trailer, Crocker," the chief said, "and we found the pills, all of the drugs."

So that was what had been keeping Dalton distracted, the "personnel matter" that weighed on his mind—Boyd Crocker.

Chief Dalton took a tentative step forward. "Now drop your weapon, Crocker. Just drop it . . . slowly."

Boyd's face began to contort. He looked as if his face was

morphing into tears. His shoulders sagged. The air going out of his body.

"Put the weapon down." Dalton raised his own pistol higher, away from his body, and centered right on Boyd Crocker.

Slowly, very slowly, Boyd began to lower the pistol. He turned to face Dalton. There was no longer any anger. There was pain, real pain. He bent forward, the arm holding the pistol sagging toward the floor.

He let the pistol drop with a thud.

"Now kick it away," Dalton commanded.

Boyd moved his right foot in a short kicking motion. He missed the pistol and tried it again. The pistol scooted away from him and Lib grabbed it up quickly.

Dalton holstered his weapon and approached Boyd. "Put your hands behind your back," he said softly.

When Boyd Crocker was cuffed with his hands behind his back, Officer Bingham exhaled audibly and joined the chief in taking one of Boyd's elbows to lead him away.

"I'll go with you," Lib said. She scurried to retrieve her jacket and utility belt.

Chief Dalton turned toward Mary Ann, David, and Elise. "All of you all right?"

They nodded.

"I'll need statements from all of you," Dalton said, "but not tonight. Tomorrow."

David followed Lib a few steps. "Lib, can I go with you?"

She stopped, reached one hand out for his arm. "No . . . no, thanks. But, David," she said, "you saved us all. You saved us." Then, "I'll see you later."

"Most certainly," he said.

The three left in the center of the stage looked at each other. There were efforts at smiles, as if congratulating themselves on still being alive. David rubbed his right elbow, then flexed the fingers of his left hand as if trying to recover feeling.

Mary Ann saw the front door of the theater open and Thaddeus rushing down the aisle toward the stage. He bounded up the steps. "Police scanner," he said as a way of explanation. Then, "I saw Chief Dalton leading him away. Thank God you are all okay."

He came to Mary Ann and enfolded her in his arms. She stood there trembling. But it felt so good to be in his arms. She rested her head against his chest and breathed him in. *I'm so glad you are here, you ol' rumpled skeptic you.*

CHAPTER THIRTY-FIVE

It was less than three weeks that the DNA came back, and positively identified the skin found under Jamie Driscoll's fingernails to Boyd Crocker. This put the lock on Crocker, who remained in jail awaiting trial. Thaddeus theorized that Crocker would probably plea second-degree murder, not premeditated, for fewer years. "But I wonder if he'll survive in prison," Thaddeus had said. "I mean there will be those in there who will take a very dim view of a former police officer who may have been responsible for their arrest."

He also said that Chief Dalton had, indeed, been suspicious of Crocker. That suspicion constituted the concern over "personnel matters" that Dalton wrestled with.

The play *Boeing Boeing*, produced by The Other Side of the Tracks Community Theater, went extremely well, with four performances over two weekends just before Thanksgiving.

After the very first performance, the entire cast took bows; then Elise had David, Phillip, and Mary Ann come out as a trio. And, at Elise's insistence, just Mary Ann took a bow. The audience came to their feet and Thaddeus was right there in the front row, applauding. Mary Ann smiled at him.

It was just before Christmas when the first real kiss occurred.

Thaddeus had asked Mary Ann to go to dinner with him at Russo's down at the Outer Banks. The meal was excellent, and prepared by owner/chef Joey Russo, who bounded out to speak to them while they were finishing their meal.

When Thaddeus brought Mary Ann home, he walked her to the door and they stepped inside the foyer. They stood there a little awkwardly for a moment. Mary Ann told him for the third or fourth time how much she had enjoyed the evening, and then Thaddeus took her hand and asked if he could kiss her good night. She said yes, and she looked up at him and rose just a little bit on her toes.

Maybe she thought it would be a rather chaste kiss, and maybe he did too. But when they started, it kept going, and she felt her heart beating faster and he held her closer and closer and their lips parted and she could feel him against her and she pushed back against him.

The kiss ended with both of them looking into each other's eyes, as if they didn't know what to think, as if they were startled.

Mary Ann, her breath coming a little fast, said, "Oh, my . . . and we've got to work together."

He gave the barest nod of his head. "It'll be all right," he managed to say.

They said good night, and he left. Mary Ann watched him drive away, still savoring the kiss. This was a new beginning and they could never undo it.

On Monday, at the newspaper, they tried to act like nothing had happened. Thaddeus talked about the upcoming meeting in Raleigh of the North Carolina Press Association and how he thought the *Camford Courier* would probably be a candidate for multiple awards.

"I want you to go with me," he said.

She of course said she would be happy to attend.

Three weeks later she packed for the overnight trip to Raleigh. Mary Ann had her small suitcase opened on her bed. She couldn't decide whether to put the little black dress in the suitcase or keep it on a hanger for the back of Thaddeus's truck. She decided to fold it neatly and put it in the suitcase. It would shake out without wrinkles.

She was about finished packing when she opened the third drawer of her dresser and took out the new pajamas she had bought at the Outer Banks that Sunday with Elise. They still had the white tissue around them.

She smiled to herself as she laid the pajamas on the top of everything else in the suitcase.

Maybe I won't need these.

The smile began to grow, and a hint of a mischievous twinkle developed in her eyes.

Well, just maybe . . .

-The End-

CPSIA information can be obtained
at www.ICGtesting.com
Printed in the USA
FFOW02n1503140618
471071213-49590FF

9 781622 681396